Just perfect.

We piled into the VW, which sputtered and spit as Sumner tried to negotiate our cul-de-sac. The VW was old and faded blue and had a distinctive rattling purr to it that I could pick out anywhere. It woke me up when he dropped Ashley off late at night or cruised by just to see the light in her window. Sumner called it his theme music.

The trip to the beach was about four hours, and of course going down the highway in a convertible, you can't hear anything going on in the front seat. So I just sat back and stared up at the sky as the sun went down and it got dark. Once we turned off onto the smaller roads that wound up along the Virginia coast, Sumner turned up the radio and found nothing but beach music, so we sang along, making up our own words when we didn't know the real ones. The engine was puttering and my sister was laughing and the stars were so bright above us, constellations swirling. It was just perfect, just right all at once.

NOVELS BY SARAH DESSEN

That Summer

Someone Like You

Keeping the Moon

Dreamland

This Lullaby

The Truth About Forever

that summer

SARAH DESSEN

speak
An Imprint of Penguin Group (USA) Inc.

I would like to acknowledge Doris Betts and Jill McCorkle, my teachers, for their support; Dannye Romine Powell, for granting permission for me to use the wonderful poem that inspired this book; my agent, Leigh Feldman; and Lee Smith, for her friendship, generosity, and practical wisdom. Thank you.

SPEAK
Published by Penguin Group
Penguin Group (USA) Inc.,
345 Hudson Street, New York, New York 10014, U.S.A.
Penguin Books Ltd, 80 Strand, London WC2R ORL, England
Penguin Books Australia Ltd, 250 Camberwell Road, Camberwell, Victoria 3124, Australia
Penguin Books Canada Ltd, 10 Alcorn Avenue, Toronto, Ontario, Canada M4V 3B2
Penguin Books (N.Z.) Ltd, 182-190 Wairau Road, Auckland 10, New Zealand

First published in the United States of America by Orchard Books, 1996
Published by Puffin Books, a division of Penguin Putnam Inc., 1998
This edition published by Speak, an imprint of Penguin Group (USA) Inc., 2004

19 18

Text copyright © Sarah Dessen, 1996

The poem "At Every Wedding Someone Stays Home"
is used by permission of the author, Dannye Romine Powell.

THE LIBRARY OF CONGRESS HAS CATALOGED THE PUFFIN EDITION AS FOLLOWS:
Dessen, Sarah.
That summer \ Sarah Dessen.
p. cm.
Summary: During the summer of her divorced father's remarriage and her sister's wedding,
fifteen-year-old Haven comes into her own by letting go of the myths of the past.
ISBN 0-14-038688-2
[1. Sisters—Fiction. 2. Interpersonal relations—Fiction. 3. Weddings—Fiction.] I. Title.
PZ7.D455 Th 1988 [Fic]—dc21 97-50534 CIP AC

Speak ISBN 0-14-240172-2

Printed in the United States of America

To my parents, for their faith and patience,

and to Jay, for everything else

At Every Wedding Someone Stays Home

This one sits all morning
beside the picture window,
staring out at the lawn
which in these situations
is always under a sheet of ice,
even in June. The girl is wearing
her quilted robe, gloves,
fur-lined slippers. Still she can't
get warm. Her mother gets hot
just watching her, so she goes out
for groceries, makes a great show
when she returns of rattling
the brown paper bags she saves
to line the bird cage.
Now she is running water,
peeling melons, humming, arranging
daisies. We who are watching
want the mother to quit making noise,
to stop chopping fruit, to leave
the kitchen. We want her to walk
down the hall to the closet
where the wool blankets are stored.
We want her to gather five or six,

the solids, the stripes,
the MacGregor plaids and tuck them
under her daughter's legs, saving one
for her feet and one for her thin shoulders.
Now we want her to heat water for tea,
bring in wood and quick
before her daughter freezes
seal all the windows
against the stray, chill peal of bells.

—Dannye Romine Powell

that summer

Chapter One

*It's funny how one summer can change every-
thing. It must be something about the heat and the
smell of chlorine, fresh-cut grass and honeysuckle,
asphalt sizzling after late-day thunderstorms, the
steam rising while everything drips around it.
Something about long, lazy days and whirring air
conditioners and bright plastic flip-flops from the
drugstore thwacking down the street. Something
about fall being so close, another year, another
Christmas, another beginning. So much in one
summer, stirring up like the storms that crest at
the end of each day, blowing out all the heat and
dirt to leave everything gasping and cool. Everyone
can reach back to one summer and lay a finger
to it, finding the exact point when everything
changed. That summer was mine.*

The day my father got remarried, my mother was up at
six A.M. defrosting the refrigerator. I woke to the sound
of her hacking away and the occasional thud as a huge
slab of ice crashed. My mother was an erratic defroster.
When I came down into the kitchen, she was poised in
front of the open freezer, wielding the ice pick, Barry
Manilow crooning out at her from the tape player she

kept on the kitchen table. Around Barry's voice, stacked in dripping piles, were all of our perishables, sweating in the heat of another summer morning.

"Oh, good morning, Haven." She turned when she saw me, wiping her brow with the ice pick still in hand, making my heart jump as I imagined it slipping just a bit and taking out her eye. I knew that nervous feeling so well, even at fifteen, that spilling uncontrollability that my mother brought out in me. It was as if I was attached to her with a tether, her every movement yanking at me, my own hands reaching to shield her from the dangers of her waving arms.

"Good morning." I pulled out a chair and sat down next to a stack of packaged chicken. "Are you okay?"

"Me?" She was back on the job now, scraping. "I'm fine. Are you hungry?"

"Not really." I pulled my legs up to my chest, pressing hard to fold myself into the smallest size possible. It seemed like every morning I woke up taller, my skin having stretched in the night while I slept. I had dreams of not being able to fit through doors, of becoming gigantic, towering over people and buildings like a monster, causing terror in the streets. I'd put on four inches since April, and showed no signs of letting up. I was already five-eleven, with only a few more little lines on the measuring stick before six feet.

"Haven." My mother looked at me. "Please don't sit that way. It's not good for you and it makes me nervous." She stood there staring at me until I let my legs drop. "That's better." Scrape, scrape. Barry sang on, about New England.

I still wasn't sure what had brought me down from my bed so early on a Saturday, aside from the noise of my mother loosening icebergs from our Frigidaire. I hadn't slept well, with my dress for the wedding hanging from the curtain rod, fluttering in the white light of the street lamp outside my window. At two P.M. my father was marrying Lorna Queen, of "Lorna Queen's Weather Scene" on WTSB News Channel 5. She was what they called a meteorologist and what my mother called the Weather Pet, but only when she was feeling vindictive. Lorna was blond and perky and wore cute little pastel suits that showed just enough leg as she stood smiling in front of colorful maps, sweeping her arm as if she controlled all the elements. My father, Mac McPhail, was the sports anchor for channel five, and he and the Weather Pet shared the subordinate news desk, away from the grim-faced anchors, Charlie Baker and Tess Phillips, who reported real news. Before we'd known about my father's affair with the Weather Pet, I'd always wondered what they were smiling and talking about in those last few minutes of the broadcast as the credits rolled. Charlie Baker and Tess Phillips shuffled important-looking papers, worn thin from a hard day of news chasing and news delivering; but my father and the Weather Pet were always off to the side sharing some secret laugh that the rest of us weren't in on. And when we finally did catch on, it wasn't very funny after all.

Not that I didn't like Lorna Queen. She was nice enough for someone who broke up my parents' marriage. My mother, in all fairness, always blamed my father and limited her hostility to the nickname Weather Pet and to the occasional snide remark about my father's growing mass of hair, which at the time of the separation was receding with great speed and now seemed to have reversed itself and grown back with the perseverance and quickness of our lawn after a few good days of rain. My mother had read all the books about divorce and tried hard to make it smooth for me and my sister, Ashley, who was Daddy's pet and left the room at even the slightest remark about his hair. My mother kept her outbursts about that to a minimum, but I could tell by the way she winced when they showed my father and Lorna together at their subordinate news desk that it still hurt. Before the divorce my mother had been good at outbursts, and this quietness, this holding back, was more unnerving than I imagined any breakdown could be. My mother, like Ashley, has always cultivated the family dramatic streak, started by my grandmother, who at important family gatherings liked to fake horrible incidents if she felt she was not getting enough attention. No reunion, wedding, or funeral was complete without at least one stroke, heart attack, or general collapse from Grandma at which time everyone shifted into High Dramatic Mode, fussing and running around and generally creating the kind of chaos that my family is well known for.

This always made me kind of nervous. I hadn't inherited that flair for the stage that Ashley and my mother had, this snap ability to lose control in appropriate instances. I was more like my father, steady and worried all the time. Back then, we had it down to a science:

Mom and Ashley overreacting, thriving on crisis, my father and I standing calm, together, balancing them out. Then my father left, and like a table short a leg, things had been out of whack ever since.

"So are you going?" That was Ashley, standing in the kitchen doorway in a T-shirt and socks. Just looking at her made me acutely aware of my own height, the pointedness of my elbows and hipbones, the extra inch I'd put on in the last month. At twenty-one my sister is a petite five-four, with the kind of curvy, rounded body that I wish I'd been born with; tiny feet, perfect hair, small enough to be cute, but still a force to be reckoned with. At my age she had already been voted Most Popular, dated (and dumped) the captain of the football team, and been a varsity cheerleader. She was always the one at the top of the pyramid, tiny enough to be passed from hand to hand overhead until she stood high over everyone else, a bit shaky but triumphant, before letting loose and tumbling head over heels to be caught at the bottom with a sweep of someone's arms. I remembered her in her cheerleading uniform, short blue skirt, white sweater, and saddle shoes, grabbing her backpack to run out to a carful of teenagers waiting outside, squealing off to school with a beep of the horn. Back then, Ashley seemed to live a life just like Barbie's: popular and perfect, always with a handsome boyfriend and the cool crowd. All she needed was the Dreamhouse and a purple plastic Corvette to make it real.

Now, my sister just scowled at me when she caught me looking at her, then scratched one foot with the other. She had a good tan already, and on the inside of her left ankle I could see the yellow butterfly tattoo she'd gotten in Myrtle Beach when she'd gotten drunk after high school graduation two years earlier and someone double dared her. Ashley was wild, but that was before she got engaged.

"No. I don't think I should go," my mother said. "I think it's in bad taste."

"Go where?" I said.

"She invited you," Ashley said, yawning. "She wouldn't have done that if she didn't want you there."

"Where?" I said again, but of course no one was listening to me. There was another crash as a block of ice fell out of the freezer.

"I'm not going," my mother said solidly, planting a hand on her hip. "It's tacky and I won't do it."

"So don't do it," Ashley said, coming into the kitchen and reaching across me to pick up a pack of frozen waffles from the table.

"Do what?" I said again, louder this time because in our house you have to make a commotion to even be heard.

"Go to your father's wedding," my mother said. "Lorna sent me an invitation."

"She did?"

"Yes." This fell into the category of whether Lorna, the Weather Pet, was either downright mean or just stupid. She did a lot of things that made me question this, from telling me it was okay to call her Mom once she married my father to sending my mother a framed picture of an old family Christmas card she'd found among my dad's junk. We'd all sat around the kitchen table, staring at it, my mother holding it in one hand with a puckered look on her face. She'd never said a word about it, but instead went outside and ripped up weeds in the garden for forty-five minutes, handful after handful flying over her head in a massive horticultural tantrum. I believed Lorna was mostly mean, bordering on stupid; my mother refused to even voice an opinion; and because Ashley couldn't bear to criticize anything about Daddy she said Lorna was just stupid and left mean out of it altogether. All I knew was that I would never call a woman only five years older than Ashley Mom and that that framed Christmas card was what Ann Landers would call In Quite Poor Taste.

So my mother was not with us as we set off for the church that afternoon, in our matching shiny pink bridesmaid dresses, to see our father be bonded in holy matrimony to this probably stupid but quite possibly just mean Weather Pet. I'd felt sorry for my mother as she lined us up in front of the mantel to take a picture with her little Instamatic, cooing about how lovely we looked. She stood in the doorway behind the screen, waving as we walked out to the car, the camera dangling from her wrist, and I realized suddenly why Ashley might have wanted her to come, even if it was tacky. There was something so sad about leaving her behind, all of a sudden, and I had an urge to run back and take her with me, to pull that tether tight and hold her close. But I didn't, like I always don't, and instead climbed into the car next to Ashley and watched my mother waving as we pulled away from the house. At every wedding someone stays home.

* * *

As we got out of the car at the church, I saw Ashley's fiancé, Lewis Warsher, heading our way from the other end of the lot where he'd parked his little blue Chevette. He was fixing his tie as he walked, because Lewis was a neat dresser. He always wore shiny shoes and skinny ties in pastel colors. When Ashley saw him I swear she shrank about two inches; there is something about Lewis that turns my sister, who is tough as nails, into a swooning, breathless belle.

"Hey, honey." And of course they were immediately connected, his arms slipping around her small waist, pulling her close for one of those long, emotional hugs where it looked like he was the only thing that was keeping her from collapsing to the ground. Ashley and Lewis spent a lot of time hugging each other, supporting each other physically, and whispering. They gave me a complex, always with their heads together murmuring in corners of rooms, their voices too low to catch anything but a few vowels.

"Hey," Ashley whispered. They were still hugging. I stood there fiddling with my dress; I had no choice but to wait. Ashley hadn't always been this way; she'd had boyfriends for as long as I could remember, but none of them had affected her like Lewis. For years we kept track of major family events by who Ashley had been dating at the time. During the Mitchell period, I got my braces and Grandma came to live with us. The Robert era included my mother going back to night school and Ashley getting in the car wreck that broke her leg and made her get the stitches that left a heart-shaped scar on her right shoulder. And it was during the year-long Frank ordeal that the divorce came down, complete with law proceedings, family therapy, and the advent of Lorna, the Weather Pet. It was a boyfriend timeline: I could not remember dates, but I could place each important event in my life with a face of a boy whose heart Ashley had broken.

But this was all before Lewis, whom Ashley met at the Yogurt Paradise at the mall where they both worked. Ashley was a Vive cosmetics salesgirl, which meant she stood behind a big counter in Dillard's department store, wearing a white lab coat and putting overpriced makeup on rich ladies' faces. She thought she was something in that lab coat, wearing it practically everywhere like it meant she was a damn doctor or something. She was just coming out of the messy breakup of the Frank era and was consoling herself with a yogurt sundae when Lewis Warsher sensed her pain and sat himself down at her table because she looked like she needed a friend. These are their words, which I know because I've heard this story entirely too many times since they announced their engagement six months ago.

My mother said Ashley missed our father, and needed a protective figure; Lewis just came along at the right time. And Lewis *did* protect her, from old boyfriends and gas station attendants and bugs that dared to cross her path. Still, sometimes I wondered what she really saw in him. There was nothing spectacular about Lewis, and it was a little unsettling to see my sister, whom I'd always admired for being plucky and tough and not taking a bit of lip off anyone, shrinking into his arms whenever the world rose up to meet her face to face.

"Hey, Haven." Lewis leaned over and pecked me on the cheek, still holding Ashley close. "You look beautiful."

"Thanks," I said. Lewis had the arm clamp on Ashley, steering her towards the church, with me following. Even though we were wearing the same god-awful pink fluffy dresses, we looked totally different. Ashley was a short, curvy pink rose, and I was a tall, pink straw, like something you'd plunk down in a big fizzy drink. This was the kind of thing I was always thinking about since my body betrayed me and made me a giant.

When I was in first grade I had a teacher named Mrs. Thomas. She was young, sported a flip hairdo that made her look just like Snow White, smelled like Lily of the Valley, and kept a picture of a man in a uniform on her desk, staring stiffly out from the frame. And even though I was shy and slow at math, she didn't care. She loved me. She'd come up beside me in the lunch line or during story hour and smooth her hand over my head, saying "Why, Miss Haven, you're just no bigger than a minute." I was compact at six, able to fit neatly into small places that now were inaccessible: under the crook of an arm, in the palm of a hand. At five-eleven and counting, I no longer had the sense that someone like Mrs. Thomas could neatly enclose me if danger should strike. I was all bony elbows and acute angles, like a jigsaw puzzle piece that can only go in the middle, waiting for the others to fit around it to make it whole.

The church was filling up with people, which wasn't surprising: my father is the kind of person who knows everybody, somehow. Mac McPhail, sportscaster, beer drinker, teller of tall tales and big lies, the latter being told mostly to my mother in the last few months of the marriage. I can remember sitting in front of the TV watching my father on the local news every night, seeing the sly sideways looks he and Lorna Queen exchanged during the leads into commercial breaks, and still not having any idea that he would leave my mother for this woman best known for her short skirts and pouty-lipped way of saying "upper-level disturbance." She didn't know the half of it. There had been no disturbance before like the one that hit our house the day my father came home from the station, sat my mother down at the kitchen table right under the vent that leads to the floor beneath the counter in my bathroom, and dropped the bomb that he'd fallen hard for the Weather Pet. I sat on the side of my tub, toothbrush in hand, and wished the house had been designed differently so I wouldn't have been privy to this most painful of moments. My mother was silent for a long time, my father's voice the only one wafting up through the floor, explaining how he couldn't help it, didn't want to lie anymore, had to come clean, all of this with his booming sportscaster voice, so agile at curving around scores and highlights, stumbling over the simple truth that his marriage was over. My mother started crying, finally, and then told him to leave in a quiet, steady voice that made the room seem suddenly colder. Two weeks later he had moved into the Weather Pet's condo. He met me and

Ashley for lunch each Saturday and took us to the beach every other weekend, spending too much money and trying to explain everything by putting his arm around my shoulder, squeezing, and sighing aloud.

But that had been a year and a half ago, and now here it was wedding day, the *first* wedding I was dreading this summer. We walked into the lobby of the church and were immediately gathered up in the large arms of my aunt Ree, who was representing the bulk of my father's side of the family, most of whom were still upset about the divorce and sided with my mother, family loyalty notwithstanding. But Aunt Ree was ample enough to represent everyone in her flowing pink muu-muu, a corsage the size of a small bush pinned to her chest.

"Haven, you come over here and give your aunt Ree some sugar." She squashed me against her, and I could feel the flowers poking into my skin. She'd clamped Ashley in her other arm, somehow getting her away from Lewis, and hugged us both as tightly together as if she was trying to consolidate us into one person. "And Ashley, this should all seem pretty familiar to you. When's your big day again?"

"August nineteenth," Lewis said quickly. I wondered if that was the answer he gave to any question now. It was what I usually said.

Aunt Ree pushed me back, holding me by both arms as Ashley made a quick dash back to Lewis. "Now you are just growing like a weed, I swear to God. Look at you. How tall are you?"

I smiled, fighting the urge to slouch. "Too tall."

"No such thing." She tightened her grip on my arm. "You can never be too tall or too thin. That's what they say, isn't it?"

"It's too rich or too thin." Ashley said. Leave it to my short, curvy sister to correct even a misworded compliment.

"Whatever," Aunt Ree said. "You're beautiful, anyway. But we're running late and the bride is a mess. We've got to go find you your bouquets."

Ashley kissed Lewis and clung to him for a few more seconds before following me and Aunt Ree through the masses of perfumed wedding guests to a side door that led into a big room with bookcases covering all four walls. Lorna Queen was sitting at a table in the corner, a makeup mirror facing her, with some woman hovering around picking at her hair with a long comb.

"We're here!" Aunt Ree said in a singsong voice, presenting us in all of our pink as if she'd created us herself. "And just in time."

Lorna Queen *was* a beautiful woman. As she turned in her seat to face us, I realized that again, just as I always did when I watched her doing her forecasts in her short skirts with color-coordinated lipsticks. She was pert and perfect and had the tiniest little ears I'd ever seen on anyone. She kept them covered most of the time, but once at the beach I'd seen her with her hair pulled back, with those ears like seashells molded against her skin. I'd always wondered if she heard like the rest of us or if the world sounded different through such small receptors.

"Hi, girls." She smiled at us and dabbed her eyes with a neatly folded Kleenex. "Y'all look beautiful."

"Are you okay?" Ashley asked her.

"I'm fine. I'm just"— she sniffled daintily—"so happy. I've waited for this day for so long, and I'm just so happy."

The woman doing her makeup rolled her eyes. "Lorna, honey, waterproof mascara can only do so much. You've got to stop crying."

"I know." She sniffled again, reaching out to take my hand and Ashley's. "I want you girls to know how much I love your father. I'm going to make him just as happy as I can, and I'm so glad we're all going to be a family."

"We're very happy for you," Ashley said, speaking for both of us, which she often did when Lorna was concerned.

Lorna was tearing up again when a man in a suit came in through another door and whispered, "Ten minutes," then flashed the thumbs-up sign as if we were about to go out and play the Big Game.

"Ten minutes," Lorna said, her hand fluttering out of mine and to her face, dabbing her eyes. The makeup woman spun her back around in the chair and moved in with the powder puff. "My God, it's actually happening."

Ashley reached into her purse and pulled out a lipstick. "Do like this," she said to me, pursing her lips. I did, and she put some on me, smoothing it across with a finger. "It's not really your color, but it'll do."

I stood there while she added some more eye shadow and blush to my face, all the while looking at me through half-shut eyes, practicing her craft, her face very close to mine. This was the Ashley I remembered from my childhood, when the five-year gap didn't seem that large and we set up our Barbie worlds in the driveway every day after school, my Ken fraternizing with her Skipper. This was the Ashley who painted my nails at the kitchen table during long summers, the back door swinging in the breeze and the radio on. This was the Ashley who came into my room late one night after breaking up with Robert Losard and sat on the edge of my bed crying until I wrapped my arms awkwardly around her and smoothed her hair, trying to understand the words she was saying. This was the Ashley who had climbed out on the roof with me all those nights in the first few months of the divorce and told me how much she missed my father. This was the Ashley I loved, away from Lewis's clinging hands and the wedding plans and the five-year-wide impasse that neither of us could cross.

"There." She capped the lipstick and dumped all the makeup back in her purse. "Now just don't cry too much and you'll be fine."

"I won't cry," I said, and suddenly aware of Lorna looking at us behind her in the mirror, I added, "I never cry at weddings."

"Oh, I do," Lorna said. "There's something about a wedding, something so perfect and so sad, all at the same time. I bawl at weddings."

"You better not be bawling out there." The makeup lady dabbed with the powder puff. "If this stuff doesn't hold up you'll look a mess."

The door opened and a woman in a dress the same shade as ours but without the long flowing skirt came in, carrying a big box of flowers. "Helen!" Lorna said, tearing up again. "You look lovely."

Helen was obviously Lorna's sister, seeing as how she also had those tiny little seashell ears. I figured it had to be more than coincidence. They hugged and Helen turned towards us, clasping her hands together. "This must be Ashley and Haven. Lorna said you were tall." She leaned forward and kissed my cheek, then Ashley's. "And I hear congratulations are in order for you. When's the big day?"

"August nineteenth," Ashley said. It was the million-dollar question.

"My, that's soon! Are you getting nervous?"

"No, not really," Ashley said. "I'm just ready to get it all over with."

"Amen to that," Lorna said, standing up and removing the paper bib from around her neck. She took a deep breath, holding her palm against her stomach. "I swear I have never been so nervous, even when I did that marathon at the station during the hurricane. Do I look all right?"

"You look lovely," Helen said. We all nodded in agreement. An older woman appeared, gesturing frantically. Her lips were moving as if long, unpronounceable words were coming out, but I couldn't hear a thing she was saying. As she came closer I made out something that sounded like "It's time, it's time," but she was warbling so it could have been anything.

"Okay," the Weather Pet said with one last sniff. Ashley checked my face again, licking her lips and telling me to do the same, and with Lorna Queen behind us, her sister Helen carrying her train, we proceeded to the lobby of the church.

We'd practiced all this the night before, when I'd been wearing shorts and sandals and the aisle seemed like a hop, skip, and jump to the spot where the minister had been standing in blue jeans and a T-shirt that said Clean and Free Baptist Retreat. Now the church was packed and the aisle seemed about a hundred miles long with the minister standing at the end of it like a tiny plastic figure you might slap onto a cake. We got pushed into figuration, with me of course behind Ashley since I was taller and then Helen and then Lorna, who was telling us all how much she loved us. Finally the mad whisperer walked right to the front of the line, waved her arm wildly like she was flagging a plane in to land right there in the middle of the church, and we were on our way.

The night before, they'd said to count to seven after Ashley left, so I gave it eight because I was nervous and then took my first step. I felt like the man on stilts in the circus who walks as if the wind is blowing him sideways. I tried not to look at anything but the middle of Ashley's back, which was not altogether interesting but somewhat better than all the faces staring back at me. As I got closer to the minister I got the nerve to look up and see my father, who was standing next to his best friend, Rick Bickman, smiling.

My father only does one impression, but it's a good one. He can do a perfect rendition of the munchkin who greets Dorothy right after she lands on the witch in the *Wizard of Oz*, the one who with two others sings that silly song about being the Lollipop Guild. They rock back and forth and their faces get all contorted.

My father only does this when he's drunk or when a bunch of what my mother calls his bad seed friends are around; but suddenly it was all I could think of, as if at any moment he might forget all this nonsense and start singing that damn song.

It didn't happen, of course, because this was a wedding and serious business. Instead my father winked at me as I took my place next to Ashley and we all turned and faced the direction we'd come and waited for Lorna Queen to make her entrance.

There was a pause in the music, long enough for me to take a quick glance around to see if I recognized anyone, which I didn't because all I could see was the backs of everyone's heads as they waited for Lorna to appear. Charlie Baker, Important Local News Anchor, was giving her away. There had been a long story in the paper this very morning about the novelty wedding of the sports guy and the weather girl, which went into detail about the mentoring relationship between Charlie Baker and the intern he'd taken under his wing during her first shaky days at the station. My mother had left the article out on the kitchen table, without comment, and as I scanned I realized it could have been about strangers for all the attachment I felt to my father's fairy-tale second marriage.

Lorna was beaming as she came down the aisle. Her eyes sparkled and the waterproof mascara wasn't holding up the way it should have but no matter, she was still beautiful. When she and Charlie got up to the front she leaned forward and kissed Helen, then Ashley, and then me, her veil scratching my face as it brushed against me. It was the first time I'd seen Charlie Baker, anchorman, close up, and I would have bet money he'd had a facelift sometime during those long newsdoing years. He had that slippery look to him.

The minister cleared his throat, Charlie Baker handed Lorna over to my father, and now, finally, it was really happening. Some woman in the front row, wearing a purple hat, started crying immediately, and as the minister got to the vows Helen was tearing up as well. I was bored and kept glancing around the church, wondering what my mother would think of all this, a fancy church and a long walk down the aisle, pomp and circumstance. My parents were married in the Party Room of the Dominic Hotel in Atlantic City, with only her mother and his parents in attendance, along with a few lost partygoers who stumbled in from a bar mitzvah a couple of doors down. It was low-key, just what they needed, seeing that my mother's father disapproved and refused to attend and my father's family couldn't afford much more than the Party Room for a couple of hours, a cake, and a cousin playing the piano; my father had paid for the justice of the peace. There are pictures of them all around one table together, my mother and father and grandmother and my father's parents, plus some white-haired man in Buddy Holly glasses, each of them with a plate of half-eaten cake before them. This was the wedding party.

I watched my father, thinking this as he said his vows, speaking evenly into Lorna's veil with his face very red and serious. My sister began to cry and I knew it wasn't for the happiness of weddings but for the finality of all of this, knowing that things would never go back to the way they were. I thought of my mother at home in her garden, weeding under a hot afternoon sun, away from the pealing of church bells. And I thought of other summers, long before my father lifted this veil and kissed his new bride.

Chapter Two

Of *all of* Ashley's boyfriends, there were only a few that I can remember past the dates and events they represent. Lewis, of course, who would be the end of that line come August nineteenth. Robert Parker, who two months after breaking up with Ashley in my eighth-grade year was killed in a motorcycle accident. But of all of them, only Sumner really mattered to me.

Ashley met Sumner Lee at the beginning of tenth grade, before I turned ten. He wasn't like anyone she'd brought home before: Ashley was into well-formed boys, mostly athletes—wrestlers, football players, the occasional tennis guy, but that was rare. These boys with their thick necks and muscled legs traipsed up our front walks with my sister on their arms like a trophy. They were polite to my parents, uncomfortable around me, and drank all of our milk when they came around after school. They run together like a blur, these boys, their names three letters: Bif, Tad, Mel. My father liked them because he was on his home turf, with sports as a common ground. My mother eyed her dwindling milk supply but said nothing. We all pretty much saw this to be the norm, at least until she brought Sumner home.

It was right after a nasty breakup with Tom Acker, quarterback of the Lincoln High Rebels. He was skinny and fast and chewed tobacco but only when Ashley let him. When she broke up with him he lurked around the neighborhood after school, football tucked under his arm like Ann Boleyn's head, haunting.

But Sumner wasn't an athlete. He was skinny and smooth, with black curly hair and bright blue eyes that almost didn't seem real. He had a long, lazy Alabama accent and wore tie-dyes and beat-up Converse high-tops that thwacked when he walked. Sumner was the kind of person that you wanted to sit with in the sun and spend the day. He was interesting and hysterically funny and it just seemed like if you tagged along with him you'd never be bored because he never was. My mother said that Sumner was the kind of person that things just happen to, and she was right. Weird, amazing, incredible things. He led a charmed life, always stumbling into something interesting totally by accident.

One time right after he and Ashley started dating,

he took us to the mall because he had to buy a shoe tree for his father for his birthday. We were walking along looking for one when we bumped into this camera crew filming one of those taste-test commercials right there in front of Cheeseables, the gourmet cheese shop where they also sell that snobby expensive coffee. They had some guy tasting a piece of cheese and they were trying to get him to say something snazzy they could film for the commercial, but he was hemming and hawing and spending too much time staring at the camera.

"So you like the cheese?" a woman holding a clipboard said to him, prodding. "Would you say it's the best cheese you've ever eaten?"

"Well, it's good," the guy said real slowly, "but I've had better when I was abroad."

"But it's still pretty good?" the woman asked while the cameraman rolled his eyes. "Maybe the best you've eaten in a while?"

"It's good," the guy said. "I mean, I like it fine but I wouldn't say—"

"Just say it," the cameraman said in a low, growly voice. "Just say it's the best damn cheese you've ever eaten."

The man nibbled at the cheese a little more, taking his time. The woman with the clipboard glanced around, looking for other prospective participants, and all of a sudden Sumner says in this loud, happy voice, "This is the *best cheese* I've ever eaten!" And then he just smiled a big cheese-loving smile while the onlookers watched him and Ashley turned bright red and socked him in the stomach for saying anything in the first place. That was the thing about Ashley; she loved Sumner's craziness, but it embarrassed her no end.

The woman with the clipboard walked over to us and looked at Sumner. "Can you say that again?"

"This is the *best cheese* I've ever eaten!" He said this in the same bouncy voice and added for extra effect, "I swear."

The woman turned around and gestured to the cameraman. He made fast business of shooing the first cheese guy away and setting up a fresh plate for Sumner, who grinned at us as he was escorted behind the makeshift counter and took his place in front of the camera.

"I don't believe this," Ashley said to me.

The cameraman was talking to Sumner, who was nodding and saying at random intervals, "This is the *best cheese* I've ever eaten!" as if anyone was not clear on that point yet. They set him up with the cheese, which he took hesitantly at first, nibbled with an inquisitive look, and then let a big smile slowly work its way across his face before saying as if it had just popped into his head, with clear intonation and stress on all the right syllables, "THIS is the BEST CHEESE I have EVER eaten."

The woman with the clipboard smiled, the cameraman shook Sumner's hand, and everyone applauded except for Ashley, who just shook her head. Sumner collected a bunch of free cheese samples and gave them his name and number and signed an autograph for a little boy who had seen the whole thing.

We went on and got the shoe tree and thought little else about it, except that Sumner made it his signature line and said it whenever the mood struck him whether or not there was cheese in the vicinity. Then one evening we were all watching "Jeopardy!" and, right after we'd cleared a category on water fowl, who pops up on screen but Sumner, with his cheese and his big grin and of course the line, which was by that point known to the entire family and a few neighbors, all of whom called to make sure we'd seen the commercial. And suddenly, Sumner was the famous Cheeseables cheese guy. His tag line became very cool and they had him back to the Cheeseables in the mall to sign autographs and pose for pictures, and there was even talk of a national campaign, which never happened but was still very exciting. It wasn't that Sumner went looking for adventure on purpose, more that it just stumbled across him. And for Ashley and me and my entire family, it was fun just to be along for the ride.

The best time with Sumner was the summer after fifth grade, when all of us went to Virginia Beach for a whole week while my dad was covering a big golf tournament there. Mom let Sumner drive me and Ashley down in his old Volkswagen convertible, since he had to come late because he was working that summer selling shoes at the mall. Old-lady shoes, really, the kind with thick, springy soles in neutral colors and supertough laces that won't break under tension. The summer before, he'd sold aluminum siding over the phone, sitting behind a counter all day convincing people to make major improvements to their homes, sight unseen. He said he liked to try different jobs every summer, just to see what was out there. At the old-lady shoe store, which was formally called Advantage Shoe Wear, he'd already won salesman of the month. The only bad thing was that he had to wear a tie to work, which he got around by rummaging through thrift shops on weekends with Ashley for the widest, brightest, and plaidest ones he could find, clip-on preferred.

I can remember the tie Sumner was wearing that afternoon just as clearly as I can remember everything about that one week at the beach that summer when things were still good in my family. The tie was yellow, with big green shapes on it that from a distance looked like broccoli but up close were actually just splotches with no resemblance to anything. He pulled up in the VW still in his work clothes with that tie fluttering over his shoulder, flapping along. Ashley and I were sitting on the curb with all our stuff out on the lawn, chewing gum and waiting on him. Ashley leaned across the seat when she got in and kissed him, slipping her hand up to unclip the tie as she did so.

Normally Ashley wouldn't have stood for me coming along with her and her boyfriend, but with Sumner even she was different. He made her loosen up and laugh and enjoy stuff she usually didn't—like being with me. When he was around she was nice to me, really nice, and it closed up that five-year gap that had been widening ever since she'd hit high school and stopped looking after me and started slamming doors in my face whenever I got too close to her. It's strange, but over the next few years when things got bad between us I always looked back to that day, when we waited for Sumner on the grass, as a time when things had been okay.

We piled into the VW, which sputtered and spit as

Sumner tried to negotiate our cul-de-sac. The VW was old and faded blue and had a distinctive rattling purr to it that I could pick out anywhere. It woke me up when he dropped Ashley off late at night or cruised by just to see the light in her window. Sumner called it his theme music.

The trip to the beach was about four hours, and of course going down the highway in a convertible, you can't hear anything going on in the front seat. So I just sat back and stared up at the sky as the sun went down and it got dark. Once we turned off onto the smaller roads that wound along up the Virginia coast, Sumner turned up the radio and found nothing but beach music, so we sang along, making up our own words when we didn't know the real ones. The engine was puttering and my sister was laughing and the stars were so bright above us, constellations swirling. It was just perfect, just right all at once.

Ashley and I had one room, my parents had the other, and Sumner took the couch in the main room, which my mother made up for him every night. The couch was against the same wall that Ashley's bed was, and they knocked at each other through the wall all night because Sumner was sure they could make up a code and communicate, even though Ashley spent most of the time knocking just whatever and then opening the door and whispering "What?" to which Sumner would tell her what he'd just knocked and they'd both laugh and start the whole thing over again. Ashley never laughed before like she did with Sumner; she'd always been kind of pouty and quiet, always with a stomachache or some ailment, real or imagined. But Sumner made her happy and shiny all the time, her hair long and feet bare and a boyfriend driving a convertible. She became warm and easygoing, like summer itself.

When I think back to that week in Virginia Beach I can remember every detail, from the bathing suit I wore each day to the smell of the clean hotel sheets on my bed. I remember my mother's freckled face and the way my father could so easily slip an arm around her waist and pull her close, kissing the back of her neck as he passed. I remember steamed shrimp and cool, sweatshirt nights and the pounding of the waves in the distance lulling me to sleep. I remember the walks we took every night we were there, throwing a cheap Frisbee my father bought at a gas station on the way up and chasing each other across the sand in the dark, waiting for the moonlight to catch it as it sailed through the air. I remember that week in a way I can't remember anything else.

After it was over I rode back home with my parents, Ashley and Sumner staying for a last day on the beach. There was sand in my shoes when I got home and my suntan lotion spilled all out in my suitcase, carrying the smells and sensation of that week all the way back to my landlocked bedroom. Only the sound of Mr. Havelock's lawnmower in the distance reminded me it was really over, I was home. It was a different world and I sat in the quiet of my room that night, wishing I was back in the sand, with sky and ocean so close, lost in the thick of it all.

*　*　*

At the reception everyone was drinking and the band was playing and it took about ten years for me to finally locate my father in all the confusion. He was surrounded by a crowd, like he always is, his face red and beety, a drink in one hand. I waited until he saw me standing there and made a big production of putting his arm around me, always conscious of the fact that now I was edging taller than him, just a little. It is disconcerting to look down at your father, the one person you can always remember being bigger than the rest of the world.

"Haven." He kissed my cheek. "Are you finding everything you need? Did you get some food?"

"Not yet," I said. Another group of well-wishers passed by, practically yelling out encouragements. It was always a challenge to compete for my father's attention in public. "I'm really happy for you, Dad." This seemed like the right thing to say.

"Thanks, honey." He put his arm around my waist, that same simple gesture I associated with my mother. "She's really something, isn't she?"

Of course he was looking across the room at Lorna, who was surrounded by her own group of people, all admiring the ring, laughing, and looking at my father and me looking at them. Lorna was seated in a chair with a glass in her hand, fanning herself with a piece of paper. The reception was outside, under a big tent at Charlie Baker's house, and it was hot as blazes. Lorna Queen smiled at me, waggling her fingers, and blew a kiss to my father, who I am embarrassed to say pretended to catch it.

"She's very nice," I said, waving back at Lorna.

"It's real important to me that you girls are comfortable with this," my father said. "I know these past few years have been tough, but I know things are going to be smooth from here on out. I know your mother would want them to be as well."

I felt my stomach churn. I didn't want to think of her now, in this place with the white-topped tables and tuxedoed waiters and my father's new life. It seemed horribly inappropriate if not blasphemous in some way. I was trying to think about something else when Ashley and Lewis came up behind us.

"Daddy, I'm so happy," Ashley said, letting loose of Lewis long enough to throw her arms around my father. Her eyes were still red and puffy and my father didn't know that after the ceremony she and Lewis had driven around the block a few times so that she could gather her composure before going to the reception. I'd walked with Aunt Ree to Charlie Baker's and watched them make several passes, each time with Ashley wiping her eyes and Lewis wearing his most concerned expression. Now she just hugged my father and Lewis stared off across the room, holding her purse for her. Ashley kept some things to herself.

"Thanks, honey." My father kissed her on the forehead, then reached to shake Lewis's hand. "Not too long for you, eh, Lewis? Just a month or so away, right?"

"Twenty-nine days," Lewis, ever exact, replied.

"We'll be glad to have you in the family," my father said with his smooth drinking tongue, as if we as a family were still one flawless unit, without cracks and additions, the most recent of which was making her way across the room in a blur of white, throwing her arms around his neck while the rest of us stood and watched. Even Ashley, who had long been the only one who could stomach my father's new romance, looked somewhat uncomfortable.

I spent the reception listening to comments about how tall I was, everyone trying to make it sound like it was a good thing to be a giant at fifteen. I towered over everyone, it seemed, and Ashley kept coming up behind me and poking me hard in the center of my back, which was my mother's subtle and constant signal that I was slouching. What I really wanted to do was curl up in a ball under the buffet table and hide from everyone. After four hours, several plates of food, and enough small talk to make me withdraw into myself permanently, we finally got to go home.

Ashley had too much wine and Lewis drove us home, leaving her car in the parking lot to be retrieved the next day. She was talking too loudly and being all kissy with him while I sat in the backseat and thought about how quickly summer was passing. In a little over a month I'd be back in school with new notebooks and pencils, and Ashley would be gone from our house and the room she'd had next to mine for as long as I could remember. She and Lewis would be moving to Rock Ridge Apartments, off the bypass, into a two-bedroom place with peach carpet and a skylight and unlimited access to a pool that was within steps of their front door. She already had mailing labels, just sitting on her desk waiting to be used: Mrs. Ashley Warsher, 5-A Rock Ridge Apartments, with a little rose next to her name. She was ready to become someone else. She would take her dramatics and her tattoo and her legends of boyfriends to a new home, and we would be left to remember what we could as we passed by her empty room.

When we got home my mother was out in her garden. It was falling into dark and I could just see her hunched over her rosebushes, pruning shears in hand. Before my father left we had the perfunctory subdivision yard, with straight edges and our weeds whacked away from unwanted places. My mother had a few geraniums by the back door that struggled each year to bloom and failed, maybe a sprinkle of red and pink in the early season before giving up altogether. After the separation, however, my mother was a changed woman. It wasn't just the support group she joined, or her new interest in Barry Manilow, both of which she was introduced to by Lydia Catrell, our divorcée neighbor who moved in next door just about the same fall day my father moved out. Not two weekends later my mother was in the yard with a rented Rototiller and a stack of books on gardening, ripping up the ground with all the energy and abandon she'd controlled so well in the weeks since we'd found out about the Weather Pet. She bought seeds and raided nurseries and mulched and composted and spent full days with her hands full of earth, coaxing life out of the dry, dull grass my father had spent years pushing a mower over. All through the house there were seed packets and Xeroxed pictures of perennials and biennials and alpines and annuals and roses in every color you could imagine. I loved the names of them,

like secret codes or magical places: coreopsis, chrysan-
themum, stachys. The next summer my mother had the
most beautiful garden on the block, far better than the
evenly planned and scaled plots of our neighbors. Hers
stretched itself across the entire yard, climbing over walls
and across the grass, blazing out in colors that were soft
and bright and shocking and muted all at once. There
was always a huge bouquet on our kitchen table, over-
flowing, and the smell of fresh flowers filled the house
the way a heaviness had since that October. I loved to
see her out there, hair tied back and the world blooming
all around her, the colors so alive and constant and all
by her own hand.

"So how was it?" She smiled at me as I came walking
up, my bridesmaid's bouquet dangling in my hand. I
held it up as I got close and she examined it. "That's
beautiful. You know what that's called? *Polemonium caer-
uleum*. I don't think I've ever seen it used in a bouquet
before. Maybe I should try some of that next year." She
bent over and tugged at a weed until it gave way, coming
up with a poof of dirt around it.

"It was fine," I said, wondering what words I should
use to describe such an event, the details I should go
into. "The food was good."

"It always is at weddings." She reached down and
picked a few shiny leaves, rubbing them together in her
hand. "What do you think of this?"

I took them from her and held them to my nose when
she motioned for me to do so. They smelled sweet and
lemony, like the cough drops my grandmother always
gave me instead of candy. "What is it?"

"Lemon balm." She picked some for herself, pressing it to her nose. "I just love the way it smells."

I could hear Ashley laughing from the front porch, where she was sitting on the steps, leaning against Lewis. "Ashley's drunk," I told my mother, who only smiled that sad smile again and yanked up another weed. "She had about a million glasses of wine."

"Oh well." She tossed the weed aside and wiped her hands against each other. "We all have our ways of getting through."

I could have said it all right there, all the Hallmark kinds of things that I felt I should say to my mother, words of support and solidarity and comfort. But with this opportunity so neatly presented I could do nothing but follow her down the stone walk past her rosebushes and flower beds and bird feeders to the back steps and into the kitchen. She went to the sink and washed her hands, and in the suddenly bright light I looked at her in her faded jeans and flowered shirt and thought how much she looked like Ashley: her long, dark hair done up behind her head, her tiny feet that tracked garden mud across the floor. They were both so small and precise. I wondered what she'd done that afternoon and watched my mother at her sink and said no right things, only pressed those shiny leaves to my face and breathed in their strong, sweet smell.

Chapter Three

I woke up the next morning to a wedding crisis. By July I could sense one from miles off, but I didn't have to go that far thanks to the vent in my bathroom and the fact that all major family confrontations seem to take place in our kitchen below. I was lying in bed at eight A.M., already awake but staring at the ceiling, when I heard our neighbor Lydia Catrell knock at the back door and come in with a flurry of high-pitched chatter, matched by my mother's lower, softer voice as they sat at the table drinking coffee and tinkling spoons. I listened as they talked about the invitations and the guest list; Lydia Catrell had married off four daughters and was our senior advisor on Ashley's wedding. It was Lydia who arranged for the hall and the church and Lydia who recommended the flowers and Lydia who bustled around our kitchen acting important and dispensing advice, most of it welcome. And so that morning I knew even before Ashley did that she was about to have more problems from the troublesome bridesmaid.

The bridesmaid's name was Carol Cliffordson and she was twenty-one, a distant cousin who had spent one summer with us when her parents were splitting up; she and Ashley had bunked together and giggled and driven the rest of us crazy being twelve-year-old best friends. They were inseparable. At the end of the summer Carol returned to Akron, Ohio, and we never heard much from her again except for Christmas cards and graduation announcements. When Ashley picked her bridesmaids she was firm that Carol be included even though we hadn't seen her since she was twelve and even then only for that one summer. Carol accepted and then proceeded to cause more problems than you could ever imagine one little bridesmaid being capable of. It started with the dresses, which Carol objected to because they are low cut in front. Being that she is rather flat chested (although she would never admit it), she called Ashley to say they were too revealing and could she please wear something else. Lydia Catrell and my mother and Ashley all sat around for hours talking about that one five-minute phone conversation, dissecting it and discussing its issues etiquettewise, before Carol called again to say she didn't think she'd be able to attend the wedding at all because her fiancé's family would be in town that weekend and they expected her to partake in the annual family cookout and square dance. With this, it looked like we might have gotten rid of her altogether, except that the dresses (still low cut but a different style) had already been ordered and it was too late to find anyone else. This set off another round of arguing and consoling between my mother and Ashley, not to mention Lydia Catrell, who wondered out loud several times if this girl was raised in a barn. Finally it was decided that Carol would still attend the wedding with her fiancé, then leave immediately afterwards to make the square dance.

Now there was another problem. Apparently Carol had called early in the morning, hysterical, and cried and cried on the phone, saying her fiancé had decided he would not attend and neglect his own family for the wedding of someone he had never even met. They'd had a big fight and Carol had called to cry to my mother, who clucked sympathetically and said she'd have Ashley call back right away. Then Lydia came over, was filled in, and I lay in bed listening to them go on and on about it, fretting about what Ashley would do when she was clued in to the situation. I heard Ashley going down the stairs and then their voices suddenly jerked to a stop.

"What?" I heard Ashley say after a few solid silent minutes. "What's going on?"

"Honey," my mother said smoothly, "maybe you should eat your toast first."

"Yes," Lydia echoed, "have something to eat first."

Of course Ashley was suspicious. The toaster-oven

timer rang but I didn't hear her open it, only the scrape of a chair being pulled away from the table. "Tell me."

"Well," said my mother, "I got a call from Carol this morning."

"Carol," Ashley repeated.

"Yes," Lydia said.

"And she was very upset, because she and her fiancé are fighting and she said"—a pause here, as my mother prepared to drop the bomb—"that she will not be able to be in the wedding."

There was another silence. All I could hear was the sound of someone stirring with a spoon and hitting the sides of a mug. Clink, clink, clink. Finally Ashley said, "Well. Fine. I probably should have expected this."

"Now, honey," my mother said, and I could tell by the way her voice was moving around that she had probably gone to put her arms around Ashley, pinch hitting for Lewis. "I'm sure she didn't realize what a problem this would be for you. I said you'd call her back. . . ."

"Like hell I will," Ashley said in a loud voice. "This is just the most selfish, bitchy thing she could do. I swear if she wasn't in Ohio I'd go right to her and punch her face in."

"My goodness!" Lydia said with a nervous laugh.

"I would," Ashley said. "Goddamn it, I have had it, I can't take this anymore. No one can just do one simple thing that I ask them to do and this whole wedding is going to be a total disaster and it will all be her goddamn fault with her goddamn flat chest and her goddamn fiancé and who the hell does she think she is anyway calling me crying when she's ruining my wedding and she's such a damn idiot!"

Lydia Catrell added, "You'd think she was raised in a barn. You honestly would."

"I hate her. I hate all of this." There was a crash as something fell to the floor. "I don't need her. I don't need anyone but Lewis and we're going to elope, I swear to God we are."

"Honey," my mother said, trying to be calm, but there was that crazy edge creeping into her voice, the family hysteria swelling to full force. "Ashley, please, we can figure this out."

"Call the wedding off," Ashley was saying. "Just cancel it all. I'm not going through with it. I'm calling Lewis right now and we're eloping. Today. I swear to God."

"Oh, don't be silly." Lydia Catrell had obviously not seen my sister in a fit before and so did not know to keep her mouth shut. "You can't elope. The invitations are already out. It would be a social disaster."

"I don't give a shit," Ashley snapped, and I sat up in bed. Lewis disapproved of cursing and it had been a good long while since I'd heard any four-letter word snap from my sister's lips. For a moment, she sounded like the Ashley I remembered.

"Ashley," said my mother quickly, "please."

"I can't take it anymore." Ashley's voice was tight and wavering now. "I'm so sick of everyone bothering me with their stupid details and I just want to be left alone. Can't anyone understand that? This is my own wedding and I hate everyone and everything involved in it. I can't stand this anymore." She burst into tears, still babbling on, but now I couldn't make out anything she was saying.

"Honey," my mother said, "Ashley, honey."

"Just leave me alone." A chair scraped across the floor and it was suddenly dead quiet, like no one was even there anymore. A few seconds later the front door slammed and I walked to my window to see Ashley standing on the front walk in her nightgown with her arms crossed against her chest, staring at the Llewellyns' house across the street. She looked small and alone and I thought about knocking on the glass to get her attention. I thought better of it, though, and instead went to brush my teeth and listen to my mother and Lydia Catrell cluck their tongues softly, voices low, as they stirred their coffee.

I waited until this latest storm of details had died down before I approached the kitchen and grabbed a Pop-Tart on my way out the door to work. Sunday one to six is the most boring of all the shifts at Little Feet, the children's shoe store where I worked at the Lakeview Mall. It's probably the worst job in the world, because you spend all day taking shoes off grubby little kids, not to mention touching their feet; but it's money and when you have no working experience it's not like you can be choosy. I got my job at Little Feet when I turned fifteen back in November, and since then I've been promoted to assistant salesperson, which is just a fancy title they give you so you feel like you're moving up even when you aren't. The first week I worked there I had to pass a series of lessons on selling children's shoes. They sat me in the back by the bathroom with a boxful of audiotapes and a workbook with all the answers already scribbled in by someone else until I worked my way through the whole series: "What's in a Size?," "The Little Feet Method," "Lacing and Soles," "Hello, Baby Shoes!," and finally "Socks and Accessories—A Little Something Extra." My manager was a man named Burt Isker who was older than my grandfather and wore old moldy suits and kept a calendar of Bible quotes next to the time clock. He was rickety and had bad breath and all the children were afraid of him, but he was nice enough to me. He spent most of the time rearranging everyone else's hours so he never had to work and talking about his grandchildren. I felt sorry for him: he'd worked for the Little Feet chain his entire life and he'd ended up at the Lakeview Mall shuffling saddle shoes around and getting kicked in the crotch by squirmy kids.

The mall was only a few blocks from my house, so I took my time walking, eating my Pop-Tart as I went. When I got to the main entrance I stopped to put on my name tag and tuck my shirt in before going inside. I worked Sundays with Marlene, a short, chubby girl who was in community college and hated Burt Isker for no particular reason other than he was old and cranky sometimes and always nagged her for not selling enough socks. They kept track of these things, and every once in a while on a Saturday a Little Feet manager came down from the home office in Pennsylvania and set a quota for each of us on shoes, socks, and accessories. It's hard to push socks on someone who doesn't want them, and Marlene was always getting reprimanded for not being aggressive enough about it. They wanted you to *hound* the customer, and on big sale days Burt would stand behind me as I came out of the stockroom with my shoes and hiss, "Socks! Push those socks!" I would try but the customers would always say no because our socks were so expensive and they didn't come in for socks anyway, just shoes. No matter what those higher-ups at Little Feet thought, socks just weren't an impulse item.

Marlene was already there when I walked in, sitting behind the counter with a donut in her hand. The store was empty like it always was on Sunday, the mall deserted except for some senior citizens from the nearby retirement home doing their laps, from Belk's to Dillard's and back, with a pulse-check break at the Yogurt Paradise. The Muzak was playing and Marlene was reading the *Enquirer* and grumbling about Burt Isker when our first customers appeared. Because of her seniority it was always my turn when it was slow, so I got up and went over to see what they needed.

"Hi, what can I help you folks with today?" I said in my cheerful-salesperson voice. The mother looked up at me with a blank expression on her face; the father was over by the sneakers, flipping them over one at a time to check the prices. The little boy they'd dragged in with them was sitting next to his mother and gnawing on his thumb.

"We're looking for some new sneakers." The father walked over to me, holding a popular style called Benjamin in his hand. All the Little Feet shoes had children's names; it was part of the gimmick. The Little Feet chain was full of gimmicks. "But thirty-five dollars seems kind of steep. Got anything cheaper?"

"Just this one," I said, holding up a model called Russell, which was cheap because it was an ugly bright yellow-and-pink-striped style from last year that never sold well. "It's on sale for nineteen ninety-nine."

He took the shoe from me and looked at it. It was blaringly bright, especially under the fluorescent lights. "We'll try it. But we're not sure what size he's up to now."

I went to get the measuring scale, then squatted down in front of the kid and unlaced his shoe. There was a small explosion of dirt and gravel as I pulled it off, at which his mother like all mothers looked embarrassed and said, "Oh, dear. I'm sorry."

"That's okay," I said. "Happens all the time." The little boy stood up and I fixed his foot in the scale, sliding the knob on the side to see where it reached to. "Size six."

"Six?" the mother said. "Really? My goodness, he was just a five and a half only a few months ago."

I never knew what to say to this, so I just nodded and smiled and went off to look for the ugly Russell shoe in the storeroom, where we had tons of them piled in stacks. Marlene was still in the same spot, licking her fingers and flipping through the glossy pages of the *Enquirer*.

While I was lacing up the shoe, sitting on the floor

in front of the little boy, he looked at me and took his thumb out of his mouth long enough to say, "You're tall."

"David," his mother said quickly. "That's not polite."

"It's okay," I said. I was used to this by now; kids are dead honest, no way around it.

Once we'd gone through the fitting and the lacing and the pinching of toes, and we'd all watched David walk around the store in his bright, ugly shoes, blaring pink and yellow against the orange carpet, the decision was made that they were a perfect fit and affordable. I watched the father sign his credit-card slip, his script looping and neat, then slid the old shoes into the new box and handed the kid a balloon and they were on their way. Little Feet was too cheap for helium, so all we gave out were balloons pumped from a bicycle pump, with a ribbon tied around them so you could drag them along behind you like a round plastic dog. There's something depressing about a balloon that just lies there, listless. I always felt apologetic as I offered them to the children, as if it was somehow my fault.

I told Marlene I was taking a break and went down to the Yogurt Paradise for a Coke. The mall was still dead and I waved to the security guard. He was standing outside the fake-plant store flirting with the owner, who had a beehive and a loud laugh that echoed along behind me after I'd passed them. I got my Coke and walked down a little farther towards Dillard's, where a stage was set up and some kind of commotion was going on: several people running around and hammering nails and one woman with a microphone complaining that no one was paying attention. I sat down on a bench a safe distance away and watched.

There was a sign right next to me that said LAKEVIEW MALL MODELS: FALL SPECTACULAR! with a date and a time and a graphic of a girl in a big hat looking mysterious. Everyone in town knew about the Lakeview Models, or at least about the very best known Lakeview Model, Gwendolyn Rogers. She'd grown up right here in town over on McCaul Street and gone to Newport High School just like me and was one of the very first of the models, which were basically just a bunch of local girls all made up and flouncing down the middle of the mall for the seasonal fashion shows. She was the closest thing we had to a local celebrity, since she'd been discovered and gone off to New York and Milan and L.A. and all those other glamorous places where beautiful girls go. She'd been on the cover of *Vogue* and did fashion correspondence on "Good Morning America," always standing in front of some fancy store with her hair all swept up and a microphone planted at her lips, telling the world about the latest in hemlines. My mother said the Rogerses had let Gwendolyn's success go to their collective heads, since they hardly spoke to the neighbors anymore and built a pool in their backyard that they never invited anyone over to use. I'd only seen Gwendolyn once, when I was eight or nine and walking to the mall with Ashley. There she was in front of her house, reading a magazine and walking the dog. She was so tall, like a giant in cutoff shorts and a plain white T-shirt; she didn't even seem real. Ashley had whispered to me, "That's her," and I turned to look at her just as she saw us, her head moving slightly on her long, fluted neck, like a puppet with strings that stretched all the way up to God. I didn't know what was in store for me then, what I would someday have in common with Gwendolyn other than our shared hometown and neighborhood. Back then I was still small, normal, and I just stared at her, and she waved like she was used to waving and went back inside with the dog, who was short and fat with hardly any legs to be seen, like a Little Feet balloon.

Because of Gwendolyn, everyone knew about the Lakeview Mall Models. She'd talked about them plain as day in all those interviews when they asked her where she got her start, and even came back one year to judge the contest herself. Everyone in town pooh-poohed it but still went to try out when they were old enough, even my sister, who was too short and never made it past the first round. The contest had just been held a few weeks earlier there at Dillard's and my best friend, Casey Melvin, had even gone so far as to sign us both up. I could have killed her when I found the confirmation card in my mailbox, all official on pink Lakeview Mall stationery. Casey said she only did it because I had the best chance of anyone, since being tall is 90 percent of modeling anyway. But the thought of walking alone in front of all those people while they all watched, with my huge bony legs and spindly arms, was the stuff my nightmares were made of. Like being tall is what it takes to be Cindy Crawford or Elle Macpherson or even Gwendolyn Rogers. I wasn't sure where Casey got her statistics or percentages, but it had to be from *Seventeen* or *Teen Magazine*, both of which she quoted from as if they were the Bible itself. I had no interest in modeling; attracting attention, on purpose, was the last thing I wanted to do. And so the day of the tryouts, while Casey went and got cut the first round, I stayed at home and hid in my room, drawing the shades, as if just by happening, a few blocks away, it could hurt me.

Ashley went too; as a Vive cosmetics girl she was required to stand at a booth and offer free Blush n' Brush gift packs to all the contestants. She said every butt-ugly girl from five counties around had showed up with too much eyeliner and lipstick on, posing up and down a plastic runway that was set up in Dillard's Sweaters and Separates department. The paper covered it and reported that there was crying, laughing, joy, and sorrow, as there always was at the Lakeview Model tryouts since most of the girls got sent home because they were normal looking, short and round and big and small and not Gwendolyn Rogers. They picked fifteen girls who could now proudly claim that they got to go to official mall functions like the Boy Scout soapbox car display and stand around smiling with twelve-year-olds or the garden and home show and do compost and recycling demonstrations. They also got to be in the Lakeview Mall fashion shows, the first of which was the Fall Spectacular!, which appeared to be in rehearsal that Sunday.

There was a woman in a purple jogging suit who seemed to be in charge, or at least thought she was since she was walking around yelling at everyone to be quiet. The Lakeview Models were all grouped around the edge of the stage, posing and giggling and looking important.

They were wearing red Lakeview Mall T-shirts and black shorts, as well as high heels that were clacking all over the place and making a huge racket. One of them, a brunette with her hair in a French twist, looked over at me, then poked the girl next to her so she turned and looked too. I felt myself slouching and imagined myself dwarfing the Lakeview Models in their heels and lipstick, a freak among fairies.

"Girls, girls, listen up." The woman in the jogging suit clapped her hands, bringing quiet except for the *pop pop pop* noise of the staple gun a guy on the stage was using to attach giant leaves to a backdrop. "Now, we have less than three weeks until this fashion show *must* come off, so we've got to get serious and get working. As the Lakeview Models it is critical that you present the best possible image to the community."

This seemed to calm everyone down but the staple-gun guy, who just rolled his eyes at no one in particular and hoisted another leaf up on the stage.

"Now," the woman continued, "we're going to do it just like we practiced last week: you enter, walk down the center aisle, across the stage, pause, and then go back down the way you came in. Remember the beat we learned last week: one, two, three." She snapped her fingers, demonstrating. One of the models, a short girl with long black hair, snapped her own fingers in time to make sure she got it. I finished my Coke and tossed the cup in the trash.

"Okay, let's line up and do it." The woman climbed down the small steps at the side of the stage, with the Lakeview Models clackety-clacking along behind her.

Their voices and hair tossing melded into one long stream of girl, a blur of makeup and giggling and clean skin. They lined up just to the right of me and I could feel my hipbones sticking out and wanted to cut myself to half my size, small enough to fit in a corner, under a table, in the palm of a hand.

I got up quickly as they were still shuffling into order, red shirt after red shirt, curve after curve, the same white toothy smile repeated into infinity. I turned and walked back to Little Feet while the purple-suited woman clapped out the beat behind me and the first girl started down the aisle, mindful of the pace: one, two, three.

Chapter Four

Lydia Catrell had changed my mother's life. With her tan and frosted hair and too many brightly colored matching shorts-and-sandals outfits, she had brought out a side of my mother that I believed would otherwise have lain dormant forever, never shown to the world. My mother, who had spent most of her life smiling apologetically while my father entertained and offended everyone around him, had to wait until he had stepped out of the spotlight before she finally came into her own. And like it or not (and I usually didn't), Lydia Catrell had shown her the way.

Lydia was a widow, like all women from Florida seemed to be. Her husband had been involved in the plastic utensil business and her house was filled with more colorful plastic bins and spatulas and bathtub mats than you could shake a stick at. She moved in with a flourish of bright furniture all making its way up the driveway right next to ours; a pink couch, a turquoise easy chair, a lemony-peach divan. My mother went over the next day with a mason jar full of roses and zinnias and stayed for three hours, most of it spent listening to Lydia talk about herself and her children and her dead husband. Lydia was all color and noise, in her bright pink shorts and sequined T-shirts with fringe, zooming through the neighborhood in her huge Lincoln Town Car that seemed to suck up the road as it passed. Lydia blew in like a cyclone, altering the landscape around her, and my mother was pulled in immediately.

Within a month you could see the change. My mother was wearing sandals and even the occasional sequined shirt, frosting her hair, and going out every Thursday night to Ranzino's, the bar at the Holiday Inn that featured easy-listening hits, dancing, and tons of paunchy men in toupees out for a good time. My mother came home with her cheeks flushed, tossing her newly frosted hair, saying she couldn't believe she'd ever go to such a place and Lydia was such a card and it wasn't her thing, not at all, only to head right back the next Thursday. I sat upstairs and listened to my mother pour her heart out to Lydia Catrell over coffee, thinking these were things she could never share with me. She cried and cursed my father as Lydia clucked her tongue and said Poor dear, it must have been so hard for you. Ashley had Lewis and my mother had Lydia but I was alone on Thursday nights, waiting for the rumble of the Town Car in the driveway and my mother's key in the lock on the kitchen door. I couldn't get to sleep until I heard her trying to tiptoe past my door in an effort not to wake me.

The newest thing was the trip to Europe. Lydia belonged to a travel club called The Old-Timers, which was a bunch of single women over forty who got a cheap group rate by taking trips together to exotic locales, usually Las Vegas. My mother had been on one of those trips a few months after Lydia moved in. I'd spent the weekend with my dad and the Weather Pet, picturing my mother playing blackjack, seeing Wayne Newton, and going to the Liberace Museum, all of which were listed on The Old-Timers travel itinerary. After three days and four nights my mother had returned with a new white shorts-and-sandals set, winnings of about fifty bucks, and a million stories about these middle-aged women taking Vegas by storm. She said it was the best time she ever had, so it was no wonder she was interested in the trip to Europe. That was a four-week extravaganza through England, Italy, France, and Spain, with stops along the way to see the bullfights, tour Buckingham Palace, and sunbathe nude in the South of France, the latter being something my mother chose to pass on. If she went, she'd be leaving two weeks after Ashley got married.

"Just think," Lydia was saying as I came in from work one afternoon, "four weeks in Europe. It's what you wanted to do in college but could never afford. Now you have the money, so why not go?"

"I don't have the money," my mother said. "With the wedding so close and Haven going back to school too, I just don't know if the timing is good."

"Haven is a big girl." Lydia smiled at me. "Look at how tall she is, for Godsakes. She can take care of herself for a month. She'll love it."

"She's only fifteen," my mother said, and I could tell by the way she was biting her lip that she hadn't made up her mind yet. I felt bad about it but there was some place in me that didn't want her to go. Europe seemed too far away. I couldn't picture her anywhere there, except standing in front of famous landmarks from my history books. My mother and Lydia, in front of the Eiffel Tower, Westminster Abbey, the leaning Tower of Pisa. My mother and Lydia, topless in France—the landmarks were easier.

I watched my mother from across the table as she talked with Lydia. Now and then I'd catch her eye and find her smiling at me, that same smile I remembered from when times were better and my father looped an arm around her waist, pulling her in closer the way I so often wanted to do now. To scoop her away from Lydia and the rest of the world and have her all to myself—if only for a while.

Meanwhile, the wedding continued to take over our lives. It hung over the house like a storm cloud, refusing to budge, promising possible disaster at any second. Every surface from the coffee table to the top of the television seemed to be filled with small scraps of paper detailing wedding reminders in my mother's small, neat hand.

> *Bridesmaids: orders in by?*
> *Ashley meets with caterer again July 30*
> *Haven shoes, pantyhose, hair?*
> *RSVP list, final version*
> *Europe??????????????*

She left them around like clues, a way I had of keeping up with her concerns from day to day. Just like I'd sat in my bathroom and listened through the vent to her crying to Lydia all those mornings. I was only able to share my mother's concerns from a distance, unknown to her at all.

Meanwhile my father had returned from honeymooning for a week in the Virgin Islands, with a tan, more hair, and a grin that seemed pasted on that my mother noticed even from the front window when he dropped me off after my weekly dinner with him. She tossed her hair and kept whatever sarcastic comment was twisting her face to herself before she headed out again with Lydia, the Town Car's horn beeping three times to summon her off to the Holiday Inn.

And then there was Ashley, who after dealing with Carol's on-again–off-again participation in the wedding (now back on, after many tears and much long-distance wrangling and a promise that she could leave immediately after the wedding pictures were taken) was on to another crisis, this being her first sit-down dinner with

Lewis's parents, the Warshers. I sat in my room and listened to her tearing through her closet, hangers clanking, until I was summoned in to judge which dress was best.

"Okay," she said from inside the closet, where she was busy bumping around, "this is the first option." She came out in a red dress with a white collar, tugging at the hem to make it appear longer than it was.

"Too short," I said. "Too red."

She glanced at herself in the mirror, then gave up on the hem and headed back into the closet. "You're right. Red is the wrong message to be sending. Red is a warning; it just screams out. I need something that makes me blend. I want them to welcome me into the family."

Ever since Ashley had met Lewis, she had taken to using what my mother called Oprah phrases. Lewis talked the same way; he was a placater, a peacemaker, the kind of person who would hold your hand on an airplane if you were scared, able to quote verbatim the statistics about how it was the safest thing, honestly. I could only imagine what an entire Warsher clan would be like. They were from Massachusetts: that was all we knew.

She came back out in a white dress with a high neckline and a long flowing skirt that rustled when she walked. "Well?"

"You look too holy," I told her.

"Holy?" She turned and looked in the mirror, to judge for herself. "God. This is awful. Everything is wrong." She sat down beside me on the bed, crossing her legs. "I just want them to like me."

"Of course they'll like you." This was one of the rare moments since her engagement when Ashley and I were just talking, not yelling or discussing the wedding or exchanging the odd nasty look on the stairs. I talked slowly, as if one wrong word might end it altogether.

"I know they'll pretend to like me; they have to do that." She lay back, stretching her arms over her head. "But they're normal people, Haven. Lewis's parents have been married for twenty-eight years. His mother teaches kindergarten. What are they going to think of Daddy if he gets all loud at the wedding and starts doing his Wizard of Oz thing? Plus I already told Mom she's got to keep Lydia under control because they just won't know what to make of her. *I* don't even know what to make of her."

"She's Mom's best friend."

"I guess so." She sighed, bouncing her feet against the edge of the bed.

"Do you think she'll go to Europe with her?" I asked.

"I don't know." She sat up and looked at me. "It would be good for her if she did, though. All this stuff with Daddy has been harder on her than she's let on to you. She deserves to treat herself."

"I know," I said, wondering how much she'd let on to Ashley. With that one sentence, I could feel the five years between us again. "I just think with the wedding and all . . ."

"Haven, you're in high school now. You should jump at the chance to stay alone for that long. I would have. God, I would have been wild." She stood up and went behind the screen, tossing the holy dress over the top a few seconds later. "But you won't, and that's good. You won't be like me."

I thought back to Ashley's long list of boyfriends from high school, all their names and faces running together until they ended with Lewis's skinny nose and constant look of concern. I thought of Sumner again, suddenly, and saw him clearly in my mind on the boardwalk at Virginia Beach, the sunset fading pink and red and purple behind him. I heard the doorbell sound from downstairs and Ashley said, "Get that, will you please? It's Lewis."

I went downstairs and opened the door. Sure enough, there was Lewis in one of his trademark skinny ties and oxford shirts. He was holding a bouquet of bright purple flowers with yellow eyes surrounded by some creepy kind of fuzzy foliage. It was easy to get a complex from bringing flowers to my mother's house, so Lewis usually stuck to exotic ones: orchids, tulips out of season. He wanted to bring Ashley things she couldn't get at home; with my mother's obsessive gardening, that left very little to choose from.

"Hey, Lewis," I said. "How are you?"

"Good." He leaned forward and pecked me on the cheek, something he'd taken to doing as soon as the engagement was announced. I was taller than him, and this made it awkward. He still did it, though, every time I saw him.

"You want me to put those in water?" I nodded to the flowers.

"Oh, sure. That'd be great." He handed them to me. "Is she upstairs?"

I watched him go up, taking the steps two at a time. He moved through our house now with the ease of someone who no longer considered himself a guest, no sidestepping knickknacks and perching on the edges of furniture but walking easily across the floors as if he belonged there. It hadn't taken long for Lewis to feel at home; he'd come along when we needed a man in the house. With my father gone and the three of us struggling to fill up the spaces he'd left behind, it was only natural that Ashley would find someone to hold her together, to take care of things. Maybe it was the very thing I hated about Lewis—his absolute dullness— that attracted Ashley most to him. After the divorce and all the craziness, she'd needed something normal and steady to ground herself. Maybe by then she didn't want any more surprises.

Ashley always turned to a new boy when things got sticky or hard, or lonely. But she was never alone. She called the shots, easing people in and out of our door and our lives with the wave of one hand. The ones I liked and the ones I hated, they came and went at her whim with little or no explanation to the rest of us other than a slammed door or a muted sniffle that I could only hear late at night. Ashley kept it all to herself, even when she wasn't the only one who was affected.

Ashley dated Sumner all that Virginia Beach summer and into the next fall, speeding around town in the Volkswagen and laughing all the time, filling the house with noise whenever they came breezing through. Whenever Sumner was over, everyone came out of their respective hiding places: my mother from the kitchen, my father from in front of the TV, all of us migrating towards his voice and laughter, or whatever it was that made everyone want to be around him. He and Ashley celebrated each month they'd spent together; he bought her a silver bracelet with a slender heart that dangled off of it and brushed against her watchband. I could hear them in the driveway just after curfew, their voices rising up to my window, and then the putter of the VW engine as he pulled away, that low, steady murmur that filled the entire street, humming. Ashley was happy and nice to me and things were good that fall as the days turned crisp and sharp and the weather on channel five was still being done by Rowdy Ron the Weather Mon, who was overweight, more than a little crazy, and no threat to my parents' marriage whatsoever. A new family moved in down the street and Ashley had a new best friend, a girl named Laurel Adams, with freckles and a long drawl. Ashley and Sumner gave her a ride to school every day that fall after Virginia Beach and introduced her around; pretty soon she was breezing in the back door with them. Sumner imitated her accent and she and Ashley traded clothes and I hung around the edges of rooms watching them, listening to their voices through the house. Sumner would always look up and see me and call out, "Miss Haven, stop hiding and show yourself," and Ashley would put an arm around me and tease Sumner about two-timing her with me. Laurel Adams would toss her long honey-blond hair and just say "Lawwwwd" the way she always did when she had nothing better to contribute. The weather turned colder and colder and my mother packed up all my summer clothes, shaking the sand of Virginia Beach from my shorts and tank tops before whisking them off to the attic until Memorial Day.

Halloween came and Sumner carved a jack-o'-lantern that was supposed to look like Ashley but turned to mush. Ashley's had one of Sumner's awful ties hanging off of it and dangling over the porch rail. Ashley went as Cleopatra, Sumner as a mad scientist, and Laurel Adams as Marilyn Monroe in a peroxide wig and a dress that I could tell my mother thought was entirely too tight. They took me around the neighborhood, house to house, and ate my candy; I felt like I was really doing something, being somebody, with them all around me. Afterwards they dropped me off at home and Ashley kissed my forehead, which she never did, and then they were gone, puttering down the street with the light catching the blond in Laurel's wig and turning it silver. I sat up and watched my father scare the hell out of all the trick-or-treaters with his monster mask until everyone had gone home and I got sent to bed and ate candy in the dark. I was just dropping off to sleep when I heard them outside.

First the car coming up the street and pulling into the driveway, and then Ashley's voice, harsh. "I don't care, Sumner. Just go, okay?"

"How can you do this?" He sounded strange, not like himself. I sat up in bed.

"It's done." A car door slammed. "Leave me alone."

"You can't just walk off like that, Ash." His voice

was bumpy, breathless, like he was moving around the yard after her. "At least let's talk about it."

"I'm not talking." Her feet were stomping up the front steps. "Let it go, Sumner. Just forget it."

" 'Forget it.' Shit, I can't forget it, Ashley. This isn't something you can just wipe away like that."

"Sumner, leave me alone." I could hear her fumbling with the key. "Just go. Please. Just go."

A pause, long enough for her to have gotten in the house, but she was still out there. Then, "Come on." It was Sumner.

"Go away, Sumner." Now her voice broke, a sob muffling the end of the words. "Go away."

The door opened, then shut just as quickly, and I heard her feet coming up the stairs and the door to her room shutting with a click. Silence. I got up and went to my window. Sumner was in front of the house, running his hands through his hair and staring up at Ashley's room. He stood there a long time in his costume, lab coat and stethoscope, no longer looking like a mad scientist but like one who was deeply perplexed about something, or lost. I pressed my palm against my window, thinking he might see, but if he did he never let on. Instead he turned to the VW and walked the short distance of grass to the driveway, taking his time. He started the engine and noise filled the air, his theme music humming as he pulled out, paused at the end of the driveway, and finally drove away. I got back into bed and stared at my ceiling, knowing he wouldn't be back. I'd heard Ashley dump boys before on the front porch and I knew that tone, that finality in her voice. By the next morning he'd be gone from conversation, wiped from our collective memories. There would be somebody new—soon, probably within the week. My sister, chameleonlike, would change her voice or hair overnight to match the mannerisms of whoever was next. Sumner, like so many before him, would drop from sight and join the ranks of the brokenhearted, dismissed with a wave of my sister's impatient hand.

Chapter Five

Every week, my father takes me out for dinner on Thursday night. It's our special time together, or so my mother used to call it right after the divorce, a term taken straight from *Helping Your Kids through a Divorce* or *Survival Guide for Abandoned Families* or any other of the endless books that grouped themselves around the house in those first few months, guiding us along unknown territory. Each time, he pulls up in front of the house and waits, not beeping the horn, until I come out and down the walk, always feeling uncomfortable and wondering if my mother is watching. Ashley used to come along as well, but with the wedding so close she'd taken to bailing out every week, preferring to spend the time being comforted by Lewis or fighting with my mother about appetizers for the reception.

There are always a few minutes of awkwardness when I get into my father's convertible and put on my seat belt, that exchanging of nervous pleasantries like we don't know each other very well anymore. I've always thought he must feel like he's crossing into enemy territory and that's why he stays in the car with the engine running, never daring to approach the front door full-on. He usually takes me to whatever restaurant he's frequenting that week—Italian, Mexican, a greasy bar and grill with cold beer and a bartender who knows his name. Everyone seems to know my father's name, and at every place he takes me there's always at least one person just dropping by, staying for a beer, talking sports and scores while I sit across the table with a ginger ale and stare at the walls. But I am used to this, have always been used to it. My father is a local celebrity and he has his public. At the supermarket, or the mall, or even on the street, I have always known to be prepared to share him with the rest of the world.

"So when's school start up again?" he asked after a man whose name I didn't catch finally got up and left, having rehashed the entire last four seasons of the NFL complete with erratic hand gestures.

"August twenty-fourth," I said. This week we were at some new Italian fresh pasta place called Vengo. The ceilings were blue, with clouds painted on them, and all the waiters wore white and whisked around the jungle of ferns and potted plants that perched on every table and hung from the ceiling.

"How's your sister holding up?"

"Okay, I guess." I was used to these questions by now. "She has a breakdown just about every other day though."

"So did Lorna. It must be one of those privileges of the bride." He twirled his pasta on his fork, splattering his tie. My father was a messy eater, a boisterous kind of person, not really suited to the fancy restaurants he liked to frequent. He was the perfect patron, though, with his long-winded stories and locally known sportscaster face, and now with a trophy wife to match. (Lydia Catrell's term, not mine. I'd heard it through the vent.)

"You know," he said after a few minutes of silence, "Lorna really wants to spend some time with you and Ashley. To get to know you better. She feels with the divorce and our wedding you three just haven't had much of a chance to bond."

I picked at my fettucine, not looking at him. I thought I'd done plenty with Lorna, with her bridesmaid fittings and showers and all the vacations she'd come along on even before they were engaged, plunking herself in all the places my mother used to go but not quite making it fit. Thursday nights were the only time I saw my father without her, because she had to do the six o'clock news, the nine-thirty WeatherQuick Update, and the eleven o'clock late-night forecast. Lorna was a one-woman weather machine on Thursdays. I said, "Well, Ashley's been really busy, and . . ."

"I know." He nodded. "But after the wedding, once things have calmed down, maybe you three can take a trip together. To the beach or something. My treat." He smiled at me. "You'd really like her if you just gave her a chance, honey."

"I do like her," I said, now feeling guilty. Suddenly I was mad at Ashley for squirming out of dinner and leaving me to make peace with Lorna through our father.

"Hey, Mac McPhail!" some big voice said behind me, and a huge guy clapped his hand down on my father's shoulder. "I haven't seen you in a million years, you sly dog! How are ya?"

My father stood up and shook the man's hand, grinning, and then gestured to me. "This is my daughter Haven. Haven, this is the craziest son of a bitch you'll ever meet, Tony Trezzora. He was the biggest linebacker they ever had over there at your high school."

I smiled, wondering how many crazy sons of bitches my father actually knew. It was how he introduced just about everyone that dropped by. I went back to my pasta as Tony Trezzora sat to join us, his big knees rattling the table so I had to steady my water glass with my hand. I was studying the size of Tony Trezzora's neck when someone was suddenly right beside me with one of those huge pepper grinders, wielding it like a magic wand right over my food.

"Pepper, madam?"

"Oh, no," I said, "I'm fine."

"You look like you need some. Trust me." Two twists and a small shower of pepper fell over my food. I looked up at the person holding the grinder and almost fell out of my chair. It was Sumner.

"Hey," I said as he whipped another grinder out of his pocket, this one full of some white substance.

"Cheese?" he asked.

"No," I said. "I can't believe—"

Twist, twist, and I had cheese. He was grinning at me the whole time. "You like cheese, Haven. I remember that about you."

"What are you doing here?" I asked him. The last time I'd seen him was at the supermarket a few weeks after Ashley broke up with him. He'd been working in produce bagging kiwis and had trouble meeting my eyes even as he joked with me.

"I'm the pepper-and-cheese man." He twisted the grinder again, just for good measure, then slipped it back into his apron pocket like a gunslinger after a shootout. "I'm also authorized to fill your water glass, if you so desire."

"No, thanks," I said, still staring up at him while he puttered around our table, removing empty plates and at the ready with the pepper and cheese grinders, while my father traded stats with Tony Trezzora and didn't even notice him.

"How's your mom?" He glanced around at the other tables, keeping an eye out.

I was so flabbergasted at seeing him, just popping up out of nowhere with cheese for my pasta. I said, "How long have you been in town?"

"Just a few weeks." He stepped out of the way as a

short girl carrying a huge tray on her shoulder staggered by, barely clearing a fern that was balanced on a ledge beside us. "I'm still in school up in Connecticut, but I'm thinking about taking some time off. I'm not sure."

"Really," I said, as he started to back away, off to cheese another table. "You should—"

He waved, doing some weird hand signal that I couldn't interpret, pantomime in retreat. I realized I was about to tell him he should call Ashley, and thought maybe it was best that he'd been walking away and hadn't heard. She could barely handle answering the phone now, much less any major blasts from her past.

I sat and watched Sumner work his way around the restaurant, wielding his cheese and pepper mills like a professional, laughing and joking at table after table, while my father stayed lost in sports talk with the giant next to me. I kept wishing I'd said something more important, something striking, in the short conversation I'd had with the only boyfriend of Ashley's I'd ever really liked.

Later, when I'd finished my food, I went to find the bathroom and saw Sumner sitting in a back booth eating and counting a pile of money. He waved me over, scooting aside to make room for me to sit down, so I did.

"So tell me what's going on with you," Sumner said, arranging his stack of bills in a neat pile. "Besides the fact that you are tall and gorgeous."

"Too tall," I said.

"You are not." He twirled some pasta around his fork and pointed it at me. "You should be grateful you're tall, Haven. Tall people are revered and respected in this world. If you're short and stubby, no one will give you the time of day."

"I don't want to be revered," I said. "I just want to be normal."

"There's no such thing. Trust me. Even the people you think are super-squeaky-clean normal have something about them that's not right." As he said this, a tall waitress with long, shimmering blond hair passed by, winking at Sumner. He waited until she was out of earshot, then said, "Take her, for instance. She looks normal."

I watched her disappear through double doors by the pay phone. "And you're saying she isn't?"

"Not specifically. I'm saying no one is. She looks like your typical blond beauty, right? But in actuality"— now he leaned closer to me, sharing secrets—"she has an extra toe."

"She does not," I said firmly.

"I swear to God, she does." He went back to his pasta, nibbling. "Sandals. Just yesterday. Saw it myself."

"Yeah, right," I said.

He shook his head. "Well, I guess those childhood full-of-trust days are over for you, huh? You don't believe me the way you used to."

I watched my father talking to Tony Trezzora, his face pinkish from a few beers and a good session of male bonding. "I don't believe a lot of things."

The extra-toed waitress passed by again, smiling a big warm smile at Sumner, who smiled back and nodded towards her feet. I was embarrassed and concentrated on the fern that was hanging over us.

"So," he said after a few minutes, "how's Ashley?"

"She's good," I said. "She's getting married."

He grinned. "No kidding. Man, I never would have pegged her for the early-married type. Who is it?"

"This guy named Lewis Warsher. He works at the mall." I wasn't sure what else to say about Lewis. It was hard to describe him to strangers. I said, "He drives a Chevette."

Sumner nodded, as if this helped. "Ashley Warsher. Sounds like you have a mouthful of marbles when you say it."

"He's okay," I said. "But now Ashley's miserable 'cause the wedding's so close and everything's going wrong."

"Ashley's getting married," he said slowly, as if it was a different language and he wasn't sure where the syllables fell. "Man. That makes me feel old."

"You're not old," I said.

"How old are you now?"

"Fifteen," I said, then added, "I'll be sixteen in November."

He sighed, shaking his head. "I'm old. I'm ancient. If you're fifteen, I'm a senior citizen. Little Haven. Fifteen."

My father was looking for me now, having noticed I was missing for longer than it takes to go to the bathroom. Tony Trezzora, undaunted, was still talking.

I took Sumner back to the table with me, and as we came up my father smiled and said, "There you are. I was beginning to think I'd been ditched."

"Dad, you remember Sumner," I said, and Sumner stuck out his hand as my father stood up to shake it. "He used to date Ashley."

"Sumner, how's it going?" my father said energetically, pumping Sumner's hand within his own large one. "What have you been doing lately?"

"I've been in school up North," Sumner said when my father finally let go of his hand. My father believed in the power of a strong, masculine handshake. "I'm taking the semester off, though. To work and take a break from school."

"Nothing wrong with that," my father said firmly, as if someone had said there was. "Working is the best learning you can do, sometimes."

"And that's the truth," Tony Trezzora added.

"Well, I should get going," Sumner said. "My next shift starts in about fifteen minutes."

"Here?" I asked.

"Oh, no, at my other job," he said. "One of my other ones."

"Now that's a work ethic," my father said. "Take care, Sumner."

"Good to see you again, Mr. McPhail." He turned to me as my father sat back down to his now-cold food. Tony Trezzora made his excuses and disappeared to the bar, probably in search of another audience. Sumner said, "It's really good to see you again, Haven. Tell Ashley . . . well, if it comes up, tell her I asked about her. And congratulations. On the wedding."

"I'll tell her," I said. "I know she'd want to see you." I didn't know this, but it seemed like the right thing to say.

He grinned. "Well, maybe not. But pass it on anyhow. Take care of yourself. Remember what I told you." He

• 71 •

raised his eyebrows at the six-toed waitress as she swept past again, long blond hair shimmering. "See ya."

"'Bye, Sumner." I watched him walk towards the front of the restaurant and then out the door, onto the street. I thought about Virginia Beach and the ride in the back of the Volkswagen under the stars, so many summers ago. As I sat back down with my father I could have sworn I heard the soft putter of the VW, the theme music, curving above the noise and mingled voices of the restaurant, just as I'd last heard it outside my window on that night, long ago.

In the car on the way home I looked over at my father, his new hair fluttering in the breeze, and said, "Wasn't it great to see Sumner again?"

"You know, I'm not sure I remember which one Sumner was. Was he the football player?"

"Daddy." I looked at him. "I can't believe you don't remember him. You really liked him."

"Oh, honey, I liked them all. I had to." He laughed, taking the turn into our neighborhood just fast enough to squeal the tires a little bit. My mother said his personalized license plate should not read MAC, as it did, but MIDLIFE CRISIS. I tried to tell her that was too many letters, you could only have eight, but she said that wasn't the point. He added, "They all run together in my head now. There were too damn many of them."

"Sumner was different," I said. "He went to Virginia Beach with us, remember? When you did that golf tournament and we stayed in that nice hotel?"

He squinted, as if it took great effort to reach so far

back. Then he said, quickly, "Oh yeah. I remember that. He was a nice kid."

And that was all my father, with his selective grasp of the past, chose to remember. He was skittish whenever I brought up the past, our vacations, family events. He was eager to start over—brand-new wife, brand-new house, brand-new memories, the old carelessly tucked away.

We pulled into the driveway, right beside Lewis's Chevette, which was parked with the motor off and he and Ashley still in it. As we slid up beside them Ashley looked over, with a scowl that told me they were fighting and not to get involved. Unfortunately, my father is not skilled in reading my sister's expressions: he was waving at her. She just looked at him; Lewis slumped beside her.

"They're fighting," I explained. "Thanks for dinner."

My father sighed and put his car into reverse. "See you next week." He kissed my cheek when I leaned over. I waited a beat for what I knew came next. "Need any money?"

"No, I'm fine." I never took it, even when I did need it. Ashley always *said* she just couldn't take any even though it had been a hard month and her credit card was due . . . well, okay, just this once. She had it down to an art. I would have felt strange taking my father's pocket money, a twenty slipped here or there to make up for his day-to-day absence. Besides, I had my four twenty-five an hour at Little Feet, no big deal but enough to get me by. It would have been nice to have an extra bit, but whenever I felt tempted I thought of my mother's face and said no. The tether, stretching beyond my mother and out of the house, was always attached and I was ever mindful of where my obligations lay.

I stood in the driveway as my father pulled away hitting the horn twice, that happy *beep-beep!* as he turned out of sight. I started up the walk towards the door, Ashley's voice now audible without the rumbling of my father's car.

"Lewis, that's not the point. The point is that you didn't do anything to stop it." I recognized the tone, the clipped ends of each word, like speaking right into a wall. "I just didn't think you'd ever act that way. I assumed you'd defend me."

"Honey, I don't think it was as bad as you're making it out to be. They were only giving their opinion. They didn't mean it to be some kind of attack."

"Well, Lewis, if you can't even see why it was so upsetting to me, then I guess I can't expect you to understand why it bothers me that you didn't take the action that I thought, as my fiancé, you would take."

A silence, with just the cicadas chirping and the TV from our next-door neighbors, the Bensons, playing the theme song from "Bewitched." I kept walking until I was out of sight on the porch, then took off my shoes and sat on the steps.

"Well," Ashley said with the sort of finality she used whenever we fought and she was getting ready to stalk out of the room, "I guess we just can't discuss this anymore. This is a side of you I didn't know before tonight, Lewis."

"Ashley, for God's sake." I sat up. "I understand you

weren't in the mood for their input, but they're my family, flawed or not, and I'm not going to sit here and trash them to make you feel better. I'm just not." It sounded like Lewis was growing a spine, finally, right there in the Chevette.

I expected lightning to flash, stars to fall from the sky, the earth to shake and rumble at its core, but instead I heard only the slam of the car door and Ashley saying, "Then there is nothing left to discuss. I don't want to be with you right now, Lewis. I don't know when, actually, I'll want to be with you again."

"Ashley." And there it was, just as she was coming up the walk, the plaintive whine: Lewis lost his new bravado and returned to his old self. But it was too late. Ashley was In A Mood and he'd have to ride it out, like it or not, like the rest of us always did.

She came stomping up the steps, saw me, and stopped just long enough to shoot me a look. She was wearing the holy dress, and in the porch light she seemed to be almost glowing. She kicked her shoes to the far end of the porch and climbed into the swing, making quite a racket as the chains clanked before settling into a nice, smooth to and fro. Lewis was still out in the driveway, waiting in the car.

"What happened?" I asked after a few solid minutes of her heavy sighs overlaying the occasional yap of the Weavers' dog from across the street, a fat little sausage of a dog that had a bark like a duck. There was something wrong with it, some kind of vocal problem. My father had called it Duckdog, upsetting Mrs. Weaver, who liked to dress it in sweaters, galoshes when it rained.

Ashley leaned further back in the swing and waited awhile before answering, like she wasn't sure it was worth the trouble. "They hate me," she said simply. "They all ganged up on me when we started talking about the caterer and they all hate me."

The Chevette started up now, softly, and I wondered if Lewis was actually going to leave. I'd imagined him sitting all night in the driveway, sleeping upright rather than leaving angry. But there he was, pulling into the street with one last long pause in front of the house before driving off.

"I'm sure they don't hate you," I said, sounding just like my mother, who was too busy dancing with middle-aged men at the Holiday Inn to be here for this latest crisis.

"All I said was that I hadn't felt like arguing with the caterer about salmon. If it was going to be that much trouble, we'd have chicken. I mean, by this point I have to pick my battles, right? But with just the mention of the salmon issue the whole table looks at me and Mrs. Warsher says, 'If you wanted salmon, you should have pursued it. The caterer is working for you, not the other way around.'" Her voice was high and nasal, spiteful. She still had it in her.

"You fought with his family about salmon?" Now that I knew the core of the dispute was fish, it seemed less exciting. I'd expected something major, something involving sex or religion at least.

"Oh, not just salmon. Lewis decided to tell them about Carol, too. Oh, and the invitations and how the typesetter forgot to put the date the first time around. And that's not even counting what he said about Daddy."

"Daddy. What about him?"

"Well, they asked"—she waved her hand around in summary as if it would take too long to explain— "about the family and all, and Lewis tells them about the divorce, which is fine, but then he has to go into the whole Lorna thing, and the TV station thing and how she's a weathergirl and Dad's a sportscaster and on and on and on. It was just too much."

"Well, Ash, it is the truth," I said. "Embarrassing or not."

"But he made it sound so awful. I mean, there's Lewis's whole family all grouped around the table like the Waltons and he's telling them about Daddy and Lorna and I can only imagine what they'd think if they knew Mom was out dancing with Lydia Catrell. I mean, these people go to church, Haven."

"So? It doesn't make them better than you."

She sighed, blowing hot air through her bangs. "You don't understand. You don't have anyone you have to impress now. It's different when you're older. What your family does reflects on you a lot more, especially when it's as twisted as ours is."

"A lot of people get divorced, Ash," I said. "It's not just us."

She climbed out of the swing, leaving it to rock empty behind her. She leaned far over the edge of the rail and balanced her weight on her palms while the holy dress, translucent, blew around her legs. Her hair hung down over her face, hiding her mouth as she said, "I know, Haven. But no one else has our parents."

A car blew by on the street, radio blasting; a cigarette hit the pavement with a shower of sparks. Then it was quiet again, except for Duckdog's barking.

"I saw Sumner tonight," I said quietly.

"Who?" She was still leaning over, her feet dangling.

"Sumner."

"Sumner Lee?"

"Yeah."

A pause; then she righted herself and brushed her hair back. "Really. What'd he say?"

"We just caught up for a while. He asked about you."

"Did he." Her voice was flat. "Well. That's nice."

"He's working over at Vengo," I went on. "And some other job, too."

"What's he doing back in town? I thought he was in college."

"He's thinking about taking some time off."

"Dropping out?" she said.

"No." I spoke slowly. "Just time off. And anyway he hasn't decided yet." I was beginning to regret I'd even mentioned it. Ashley had a way of taking anything good and ruining it.

"Well, that sounds like Sumner," she said dismissively. "He never was very ambitious."

"He told me to congratulate you," I answered, suddenly wanting to keep talking. She didn't have to be so nasty. "He wishes you the best."

"That's nice." She was bored with it already. She

walked to the door, reaching for the knob. "If Lewis calls, tell him I'm sleeping. I don't feel like talking to anyone right now."

"Ashley."

She turned, having already opened the door. "What?"

"He was really happy for you." She had that look on her face, like I was wasting her time so late at night. "I thought . . . I thought you'd have more of a reaction."

She shook her head, moving inside. "Haven, I'm getting married in less than a month. I don't have time to think about old boyfriends. I don't even have time to think about myself."

"I was happy to see him," I said.

"You didn't know him the way I did." She rubbed one foot with the other, that classic Ashley gesture. "Just tell Lewis I'm asleep, okay?"

"Okay."

I'd let it go now, just like I'd learned to let all things go that brought out that tired voice and impatient gesture in my sister. Being in her good graces was still important to me. I sat out on the porch for a long time, not sure what I was waiting for. Not for the Town Car, which didn't come home with my mother tucked safely inside until much later, when I was in bed half-asleep, making myself stay lucid until I heard her key in the lock. Not for Lewis's call, which came and I let ring, on and on, long after Ashley had pretended to be sleeping or was asleep. There was time for waiting, even if I wasn't sure what to wait for. It was still summer, at least for a while.

Chapter Six

There were two homecomings in the first week of August for our neighborhood. One was little, not mattering much to anyone but me. And one was big news.

The little one was the return of my best friend, Casey Melvin, from 4-H camp, where she'd spent most of the summer letting boys go up her shirt and writing me long, dramatic letters in pink magic marker sealed with a lipstick kiss. She came back plumper, cuter, and wearing a green T-shirt that belonged to her new long-distance boyfriend, a seventeen-year-old from

Hershey, Pennsylvania, named Rick. She had a lot to tell me.

"God, Haven, you would just die if you met him. He is so much better looking than any of the guys around here." We were in her room drinking Cokes and going through what seemed like eighteen packs of pictures, double prints, all of smiling people posing in front of log cabins, bodies of water, and the occasional flag. They had to salute the flag three times a day, apparently. That seemed to be the only 4-H activity involved, at least for Casey. In the mere month and a half that she'd been gone, she had become what my mother would politely call "fast."

There were at least twenty pictures of Rick in the small stack I'd already gone through, half of which featured Casey hanging off of some part of him. He *was* good looking, but not stunning. Casey was lying on her stomach beside me, naming all the people.

"Oh, that's Lucy in the red shirt. She was so crazy, I swear. She was sneaking around with one of the counselors—this college guy? And she got sent home the third week. It was too bad because she was loads of fun. She'd do anything if you double dog dared her."

"Double dog dared?" I said.

"Yeah." She sat up, plunking another stack of pictures into my hands. "And Rick called me last night, can you believe it? Long distance. He said he misses me so much he wanted to go back to camp for the first time in his life. But I'm going up there for Thanksgiving; we already asked his parents and everything.

But that's four months. I think I'll die if I don't see him for four months."

I watched my best friend, boy crazed, as she rolled on the bed clutching the stack of Rick pictures to her chest. Sometimes love can be an ugly thing.

"So what did I miss here?"

I shrugged, taking another sip of my Coke. "Nothing. Dad got married. But that's about it."

"How was the wedding? Was it awful?"

"No," I said, but I was glad that she asked. Only your very best friend knows when to ask that kind of question. "It was weird. And Ashley's practically psychotic with her wedding so close. And my mother is going to Europe in the fall with Lydia."

"Lydia? For how long?"

"Months, I think. A long time."

"God." She pushed her hair out of her face. Casey was a redhead, actually an orange-head, with that brassy kind of pumpkin-colored hair. She'd had masses of freckles when we were little, which thankfully faded as she got older; but her hair stayed basically unmanageable, a mop of wild orange curls. "Hey, who are you gonna stay with while she's gone?"

"I don't know. We haven't talked about that yet."

"Cool, the whole house to yourself! Man, that will be awesome. We can have a party or something."

"Yeah. Whatever." I tossed the pictures back to her, all the strange faces tumbling together. I didn't know these people. It was like a whole world in a different language.

She got up and put the pictures on her desk, then

tugged on her cutoffs, which dangled fringe down the back of her leg. Suddenly she spun around and said, "God! I can't believe I forgot to tell you!"

"Tell me what?"

"About Gwendolyn Rogers." She jumped back onto the bed, shaking it so madly that the headboard banged against the wall. Casey was always taking flight or crashing into things. My father called her the whirling dervish.

"What about her?" I had that image again of Gwendolyn walking her dog, the leash reaching far up to her hand.

"She's back. She came home," she said ominously (I could always tell when something big was coming), "because she had a nervous breakdown." She sat back, nodding her head.

"You're kidding."

"Her mother is friends with Mrs. Oliver, who is in my mother's walking group and was sworn to secrecy but can't keep anything quiet so she told everyone but made them all swear not to pass it further."

"So your mom tells you."

"She didn't tell me. She told Mrs. Caster next door and I overheard because I was out on the roof smoking a cigarette. They never think to look up."

"You smoke now?"

She laughed. "I have since the beginning of the summer. I want to quit, but it's just so hard. You want one?"

"No," I said, still trying to catch up with all this new information. "Why'd she have a nervous breakdown?"

"Because"—she went over to her dresser, reaching

far under the sweaters she never wore to retrieve a box with a rumpled pack of cigarettes and some matches in it—"she was badly hurt by a man. And the modeling industry. It's a hard life for a small-town girl, Haven."

Something told me these were not her own words. "What man?"

"A photographer. He took all those pictures of her that we saw in *Cosmo*; you know, the ones in that tight red sweater that showed her nipples." She shook out a cigarette and put it in her mouth, then took it out. "She was going to marry him, but then she found him in bed with a sixteen-year-old girl."

"God," I said.

"And another man," she added with a flourish, popping the cigarette back into her mouth. "Could you die?"

"That's horrible," I said. I felt guilty knowing this about a stranger, some poor girl who knew no shameful secrets of mine. With Mrs. Melvin's mouth, it had to be all over the neighborhood by now.

"She flew in last Friday, and Mrs. Oliver said she took right to her bed in her old room and slept for forty hours straight. Poor Mrs. Rogers thought she was dying of some horrible disease 'cause Gwendolyn wouldn't say what was wrong or why she came home or anything." She reached over and opened the window, then lit a match and touched it to the end of the cigarette. "She woke up at four A.M. and made pancakes, and when Mrs. Rogers went downstairs to see what was going on, that was when Gwendolyn told her. Standing there at the stove flipping pancakes at four A.M. and telling this horrible story. She ate ten pancakes and burst into tears and Mrs. Rogers said she is just at a loss as to what action to take. And since then, Mrs. Oliver says, Gwendolyn hasn't said a word."

"Ten pancakes?" I said. This, to me, seemed like the most unbelievable part of the story.

"Haven, honestly." Casey hated when anyone tried to take away from whatever story she was telling. "And that was when Gwendolyn took to walking."

"Walking?"

She puffed on her cigarette, then blew the smoke out the window, where it circled across the roof and into the sky. "She walks all night long, Haven, through the neighborhood. She can't sleep, or won't, and Mrs. Oliver says she's like a ghost passing on the sidewalk, long legged and freaky looking. All night long."

Suddenly I had chills, the kind you get during the climax of a good ghost story, when you realize the scratching on the roof is the disembodied hand or that the ribbon holds her head on. I could see Gwendolyn loping along on her thin legs, casting a giant shadow across the green lawns of our subdivision. Gwendolyn Rogers, supermodel, wandering lost on the streets of her childhood and mine.

"Creepy, huh?" Casey said, taking another long drag off her cigarette and fanning the smoke outside. "Mom says she bets modeling made Gwendolyn crazy. It's a horrible industry, you know."

"So you said." I thought of the Lakeview Models in

their pumps and matching T-shirts, posing in front of giant fake leaves. And Gwendolyn, the town's pride and joy, walking mad in the streets.

"It'll be all over the papers, and *People* magazine, soon," she went on, waving her hand in front of her face to fan off the smoke. "You know, it's big news when someone like Gwendolyn goes nuts."

"It's so sad," I said again. If even supermodel and beautiful hometown girl Gwendolyn Rogers could crash and burn, what would become of me . . . or anyone? She'd been profiled in one of Casey's *Teen World* magazines just a few months before, sharing her Biggest Secrets: her favorite food (pizza), band (R.E.M.), and beauty secret (cucumbers on her eyes to reduce puffiness after long days of shooting). And we knew these things about her, just as we did about Cindy and Elle and Claudia, girls who didn't even need last names. Girls that could have been our friends by the details we memorized about them, or the girl next door. As Gwendolyn, supermodel and Lakeview girl, tall like me, had once been.

"Casey?" There was a sudden knock on the door and Mrs. Melvin's thick New York accent, which always made her sound irritated even when she wasn't, boomed through the wall. "It's time for dinner and it's your turn to set the table. Haven can stay if she wants to."

"Just a minute," Casey yelled, tossing the cigarette out the window, where it rolled down to the gutter and caught a wad of pine needles on fire. Casey, busy running around the room spraying White Shoulders on everything, didn't notice.

"Casey," I whispered, pointing out the window at the small blaze. "Look."

"Not now," she snapped in a low voice, still waving her arms. "God, Haven, *help* me."

"Wait," I whispered, getting up and going to the window. "Don't open the door yet."

"Can you smell it?" she said, whirling around. "Can you?"

"No, but—"

Mrs. Melvin knocked again, harder. "Casey, open the door."

"Okay, okay, one second." She put the perfume on the dresser and went to the door, passing the window without noticing the flame burning in the gutter. She unlocked the door. "God, come on in then."

As Mrs. Melvin came in I was leaning against the windowsill, attempting to appear casual with my Coke in my hand and trying not to cough as a thick cloud of White Shoulders settled over me. She took one step, stopping in the frame to take two short sniffs of the air. She was a small woman, like Casey, with the same shock of red hair, only hers was styled in a bob, ends curling down neatly over her shoulders. She wore stirrup pants and a long white shirt, with huge gold hoops dangling from her ears. Her eyeliner, as always, drew my attention next: onyx black, thick on upper and lower lids, curving out past her eye to a neat flourish that made her look like a cat. It must have taken half a jar of cold cream to remove and was a bit much, especially in our neighborhood, but it was her trademark. That and her incredible sense of smell.

She sniffed again, with her eyes closed, then opened them and said curtly, "You've been smoking."

Casey turned bright red. "I have not."

I glanced out the window. The fire was still burning, looking like it might spread to a wad of leaves nearby. I had to do something, so as Mrs. Melvin crossed the room, eyes closed again and still sniffing, I panicked and flung the rest of my Coke out the window, most of it hitting the glass with a splat but thankfully enough getting to the edge of the roof where it somehow, miraculously, doused the fire. I thought we were home free until I turned around to see Mrs. Melvin, hands on her hips, looking at me. Just past her was Casey, who threw her hands up in the air and shook her head, surrendering.

"Yes you have," she said, walking past me to the open window and glancing out at the smoldering gutter. "Look at that. You're setting fires and still lying to my face."

"Mom," Casey said quickly, "I didn't . . ."

Mrs. Melvin walked to the door. "Jake, get up here." Parenting in the Melvin household was a tag-team affair. Any conflict had to be dealt with in tandem, attacked from both sides. I heard Mr. Melvin pounding up the steps before he appeared in the doorway in jeans and loafers. My father called Mr. Melvin the consummate frat boy. He was forty-three but looked eighteen and was about as whipped as any man could be. One look, one call from Mrs. Melvin and he snapped to attention.

"What's going on?" He had a newspaper in his hand. "Hello, Haven. How's it going?"

"Good," I said.

"We have a situation here," Mrs. Melvin said, directing his attention out the window to the gutter, which was still smoking a bit and thus providing the proper dramatic effect. "Your daughter has taken up smoking."

"Smoking?" He looked at Casey, then out the window. "Is something on fire out there?"

"It's that 4-H camp, Jake, where she picked up every other bad habit this summer." Mrs. Melvin walked to the dresser and opened the box on top, taking out the pack of cigarettes. "Look at this. There are probably birth control pills in here too."

"Mom, please," Casey said, "I haven't had sex yet."

"Haven," Mr. Melvin said quietly, "maybe you should get on home to dinner."

"Okay," I said. This was the way I always seemed to leave the Melvins' house, under some sort of duress. Things were always exciting over at the Melvins'. During the divorce I'd spent most of my time there, sitting on Casey's bed reading *Teen* magazine and listening to arguments and situations that blissfully had nothing to do with my world whatsoever.

On my way out the door I saw Casey's brother, Ronald, on the porch petting the Melvins' cat, a hugely overweight tabby named Velvet. Ronald was only five, not even born when I'd met Casey the day they moved from New Jersey all those years ago.

"Hey, baby Ronald," I said.

"Shut up." He hated his family nickname now. At five, he was beginning to resent anything with the word "baby" attached to it.

"See you later," I said.

"Haven?" he called after me. "How'd you grow so much?"

I stopped at the end of the front walk to face his shock of Melvin red hair and his toughskin cutoffs, the cat shedding a cloud of hair all around him. "I don't know, Ronald."

He thought for a minute, still petting. He had the freckles, a faceful plus the ones Casey had lost once she hit fourteen. "Vegetables," he said slowly, pronouncing it carefully, then added, "probably."

"Yeah." I hit the sidewalk in full stride for the one hundred and fourteen squares of cement, cracks and all, that led to my own front walk. "Probably."

I saw Sumner again later that week at the mall, during my midevening break from Little Feet. It had been a long night, too many tiny shoes to put on smelly feet, too much pressure to move the socks, always the socks. I bought a Coke and took a seat facing the stage in front of Dillard's, now complete with its fall decorations, big leaves in all different colors, with black silhouettes of glam-looking girls interspersed. I was studying the sign sitting center stage that said FALL FASHION PREVIEW! FEATURING . . . THE LAKEVIEW MALL MODELS AND FASHIONS FROM YOUR FAVORITE MALL MERCHANTS . . . COMING SOON! with a hokey tear-off calendar counting down the days, as if anyone was that excited about it.

It was almost eight o'clock, which meant I had one more hour of Little Feet before I could leave. The mall was clearing out now that it was prime time, and I tossed my cup and was heading back to the store when I saw the little mall golf cart heading erratically my way. The horn was beeping. Loudly.

It whizzed right up in front of me, dodging ferns and benches and the fountain, skidding to a flourishing stop. Sumner, the Lakeview Mall Security Man. The uniform was too big, rolled up at the cuffs, and his name tag said Marvin. He was grinning at me.

"Hey there. Want a ride?" He extended one arm across the passenger seat, "Price Is Right" showcase style. "It's better than walking."

"Are you supposed to drive people around in that?" I asked, sure I'd never seen Ned, the other guard, taxiing the help up and down the mall.

"No." He grinned. "But you know me, Haven. I call it my Chariot of Love. Now get in."

So I did. He waited until I was settled, then turned us around and hit the gas, and we zoomed down the center of the mall with Yogurt Paradise and Felice's Ladies Fashions and The Candy Shack whizzing by in a blur. Sumner was laughing, barely dodging obstacles and people, yet managing to look official whenever we passed anyone who appeared to be important.

"If we get stopped by management," he yelled at me above the whirring of the engine as we blew past Little Feet and my boss, who was selecting socks for someone, "act like you're injured. Say you sprained your ankle and I'm rushing you to help."

"Sumner," I said, but he couldn't hear me. We did another lap, slowing down a bit for the scenic tour. Sumner beeped the horn occasionally, scattering groups of teenagers in front of the arcade or pizza parlor, before finally being flagged down by a woman in a flowered dress, towing a toddler.

"Yes, ma'am," Sumner said, pulling up smoothly beside her.

"I wonder if you could tell me where I might be able to buy a personalized letter opener." She had a high-pitched voice, and the kid was drooling.

Sumner reached to the back of the cart, pulled out a clipboard, and rifled through it, concentrating. "Your best bet would be Personally Personalized." He snapped a sheet of paper from the clipboard, drew a long winding arrow on it, and said, "Here's a map. We're here"—he put a black mark on one spot—"and it's there." Another mark. "Ought to be able to find it with no difficulty." He put his pen back behind his ear as he handed her the page, one smooth movement.

"Thank you," the woman said admiringly, map in hand. "Thanks very much."

"No problem," Sumner said. I expected him to salute or something. "Have a good evening and shop with us again." And we cruised off, maneuvering smoothly through a thicket of potted plants.

"You were born for this job," I told him. We took another pass by the stage, coming to a stop by the side steps.

"I was born for every job," he said with a smile, climbing out of the cart and onto the stage. He walked to the sign in the middle and reached for the calendar, pulling the top sheet so that six days were left instead of seven. Then he stood at center stage and took a long from-the-waist bow, low and dramatic, before an invisible adoring public.

After climbing back down the stairs he jumped back in beside me and handed me the seven. "For you."

"Thanks so much."

"So," he said, shouting over the sound of the engine. "Where do you work?"

"At Little Feet." I realized how stupid it sounded even as I said it.

"Selling shoes," he said, smiling. "I did that one summer. It sucks, huh?"

"Yeah." The mall was whizzing by again, storefronts and people blurring past. Traveling with Sumner next to me, the mall was like an undiscovered country. He'd always had a way of making even the ordinary seem fun; during that summer at the beach he stayed in the water with me almost all the time, bodysurfing and doing handstands, diving for shells and making up games. Ashley spent the whole week on the beach with her towel and sunscreen, tanning, while Sumner and I swam until our fingers were pruny and white. He was the only one who had time to play with me. If Ashley pouted and made a fuss when he tried to include me, he could usually get her to come around. And when he couldn't and we fought, he had a way of taking my side without it looking like he was betraying her. He stuck up for me, and I never forgot it.

As we zoomed past the fountain I looked up at the huge banners that hung from the ceiling, each with its community motif: a house, a school, a flower, an animal that looked like a goat but I figured was a deer. I had this sudden, crazy urge to stand on the seat and rip every one of them down as we passed. I could almost feel my fingertips on the sheer fabric, smooth and giving as I yanked them from their bases. Speeding through the Lakeview Mall, dismantling it as I went. I glanced at Sumner, thinking of how much had changed, with the visions of those tumbling banners still in my head. I almost wanted to tell him, to ask him if he knew how it felt to be suddenly tempted to go wild. But we were flying along, the engine drowning all other sounds, and I let it go, for now.

Chapter Seven

After *my chariot* ride through the mall it seemed like I ran into Sumner everywhere. This was partly due to the fact that he had so many jobs. Besides pepper-and-cheese man and mall security, he was also mowing the lawn at the cemetery and driving a school bus for retarded children. Sumner did not believe in idle time.

I thought it must be fate that I kept bumping into him, some strange sign that he was meant to come back into my life and fix or change something, a voice from the past arriving in the present with the answers to everything. I knew this was silly, but it was hard to dismiss Sumner's timing.

Lewis and Ashley continued to bicker and make up, almost daily. The moods she'd made a habit of inflicting exclusively on the family were now fair game to him as well, and as the wedding crept ever closer he approached our front door as if it was a bomb and the wrong word, compliment, or even expression could cause everything to blow. My mother and I commiserated silently, watching him climb the stairs to Ashley's room like a soldier going off to battle. I found myself liking Lewis more now that he was suffering with us; I imagined it being the way crisis victims bonded, joined by the unthinkable.

It was now an even two weeks until the wedding. My mother's lists had taken over the house, yellow stick-it notes flapping from anything that was stationary and big enough to hold them. They lined the bannister, grabbing my attention as I climbed the stairs. They hung from the fridge and the television, last-minute reminders, things not to forget. They were like caution signs, flagging me down and giving a warning to proceed carefully around the next turn. The wedding, so long churning over our house in a steady pattern, was beginning to whip itself into a storm.

"Where's that other package of thank-you notes?" I heard Ashley say from the kitchen as I got out of the shower one morning. "I need more than just the six that are left in this pack."

"Well, I put them in that same drawer," my mother

answered, her shoes making a scuffling noise across the floor as she went off in search of the notes. "They can't have gone anywhere by themselves."

"Obviously not," Ashley growled under her breath, that same constantly grumbling, incoherent voice I seemed to hear behind me whenever I was in the wrong place at the wrong time.

I heard my mother come back and pull out a chair. "Here they are," she said in her singsong placating voice. "And I brought this list in so we could go over what needs doing today."

"Fine."

"Okay," my mother said, and there was a rustling of plastic that I assumed was Ashley ripping open the new cards. "First, there are the final fittings at Dillard's today at ten. I know Haven has traded shifts so she can be there, and I called this morning to make sure the head-piece was ready."

"She's probably grown another four feet and we'll have to get fitted again later," Ashley grumbled, and I stared at myself in my bathroom mirror, through the steam. I had almost outgrown my mirror, the top of my head barely within the frame. I examined myself, the geometry of my ribs, elbows, and collarbone. I imagined lines intersecting, planes going on forever and ever. My arms were long, lanky, thin, and my knees were hinges holding the bony parts of my skinny legs together. I was sharp to anyone who might brush against me.

"Ashley, you know your sister is sensitive about her height." This was the closest my mother came to scolding Ashley, who was old enough not to need it. "Imagine being fifteen and reaching six feet. It's very hard for her, and comments like that don't help."

"God, it's not like I'm saying it to her face," Ashley said bitterly, and I wondered if all those thank-you cards and all that gratitude were having an adverse effect, leaving no niceties for anyone in person. "Besides, she'll be glad later. She'll never get fat."

"That's hardly a comfort now." My mother cleared her throat. "After the fitting we can have our final meeting with the caterer. He called yesterday and said the appetizers are in order and you just have to make some final decisions about desserts."

"God, I am so sick of making decisions." A pause, during which I heard my mother stirring her coffee. "And writing these damn thank-you notes. Does anyone really think that I'm not grateful for their gift? Is it really necessary for me to state it in writing?"

"Yes, it is," my mother snapped, and I turned to look at the vent as the words came up through it, surprised at the impatience in her voice. "And I've been meaning to talk to you, Ashley, about your attitude lately concerning this wedding and those who are doing their best to make it a success."

"Mother," Ashley began in that bored voice. I could almost see her waving her hand, dismissing the words even as my mother said them.

"No, you're going to listen this time." My mother was hitting full speed now, gearing up. "I understand that you are under a lot of pressure and that it's hard being a bride. That is all well and good. But it does not, ever, entitle you to be rude, selfish, uncaring, and generally obnoxious to me or Haven or anyone else. We've been very patient with you because we're your family and we love you, but it stops here. I don't care if the wedding is two weeks or two hours away, you were never raised to behave this way. Do you understand me?"

And there it was. I stood naked, my eyes fixed on the steel grate of the vent that transmitted my mother's words, clear as bells, up to my own ears. It was quiet down there now, with only the sound of the ceiling fan creaking in slow circles.

Then, a sniffle. Another. A sob, and the floodgates opened. Ashley was wailing, her usual response to any justified attack. "I don't mean it," she began. "It's just hard, with my job and the Warshers and all the planning, and sometimes I just . . ."

"I know, I know," my mother said, having jumped back into her soothing mode, easing off the troops and letting the skirmish settle down. "I just wanted to let you know how it was affecting everyone else. That's all."

I combed my hair, put on deodorant and eyeliner, and got myself ready for work while the gushing and apologizing continued. By the time my mother had gently suggested that Ashley come up and apologize to me for her behavior of, oh, the last four months, I was fully dressed and waiting on my bed. I opened the door when she knocked, trying to act spontaneous.

"Hey," I said, making a point not to notice her red eyes and the crumpled Kleenex clutched in her hand. "What's up?"

"Well," she said, leaning against the doorjamb and rubbing one foot with the heel of the other, "Mom and I were just talking about how crazy everything's been with the wedding and all, and I wanted to come up and say I'm sorry if I've been a jerk lately. I mean, I'm sorry for taking it all out on you, you know, when I did."

"Oh." I sat on my bed, nodding. "Well. That's fine."

"I'm serious, Haven." She came in and sat down beside me. "I'm sorry. It's the last time we'll ever be living under the same roof and I've been impossible. So I'm sorry."

"It's okay," I said. "And you have."

"Have what?"

"Been a jerk. And impossible." I smiled at her. "But I'm used to that from you."

"Shut up," she said, staring at me. Then she looked down and added, "Okay. You're right."

"I know," I said.

She stood up and walked to the door, turning back to me as she stepped out into the hallway. "You know, you're going to be really grateful someday."

"For what?"

"Being tall." She looked at me, her eyes traveling from my feet to my face. "You don't think so now, but you will."

"I doubt it," I said. "But thanks for making the effort."

She scowled at me, halfheartedly, and I listened to her tiny feet patter back down the hallway to the stairs. Ashley had two weeks left in the bedroom beside mine, with a wall so thin between us that I always knew when she cried herself to sleep or had nightmares and tossed in her sleep. I knew a lot more about Ashley than she would have allowed me to if she could have controlled such things. There was a strange bond between us, however unintentional: the divorce, the wall, the years that separated us or didn't. My sister was leaving the house, and me, in just two weeks. And regardless of it all, good and bad, I would be sad to see her go.

The fitting that afternoon went the way they all had. I stood on a chair while Mrs. Bella Tungsten, seamstress, crawled around on the floor beneath me with a mouthful of pins, mumbling through her teeth to "Stand still, please." She wore a measuring tape around her neck that she could brandish in a second, slapping it against my skin or around my waist with one flick of her wrist. This was the fourth and final fitting, and we all knew Mrs. Bella Tungsten a little better than we'd ever thought we would.

"I have never in all my life seen a child grow so fast." That was Mrs. Bella, tape in hand, tugging at the hem of my dress. "It's gonna have to be shorter on her than on the rest. That's all I can say."

"How much shorter?" My mother got up from the one good chair in Dillard's fitting room and came over to inspect for herself. "Noticeably?"

Mrs. Bella tugged again, trying to make length where there wasn't any to be found. "There's nothing I can do. I can't let the dress down."

Ashley sighed loudly from the corner of the room, where one of Mrs. Bella's assistants was unfurling her train, her arms full of white, silky fabric.

My mother shot Ashley a look and squatted down beside Mrs. Bella, staring at my hemline. "No one will be looking at the bottoms of the dresses, anyway. Right?" She didn't sound so sure.

"Well," Mrs. Bella said slowly, spitting out a few pins, "I suppose. You can hope for that, at least."

Meanwhile I just stood there, arms crossed over my chest to hold the dress up, which was missing the zipper as well as the white ribbon edging and bow that Ashley had added to personalize the pattern. It was bad enough to be standing in Dillard's with my mother and Mrs. Bella tugging on my hemline and staring at my ankles; but the employee lounge was in the next room, so people kept passing through, carrying brown bags or cups of coffee and stopping on their way. They all knew Ashley, fellow employee, and stopped to coo and make a fuss over her and her dress. They just stared at me, the giant on the chair, too tall for the pretty pink bridesmaid dress that would now make me look like I was expecting a flood, not falling gracefully across my ankles as originally planned. I just stared ahead at a clock over the water fountain and pretended I was someplace, anyplace, else.

"Okay, Heaven honey, drop your arms so I can check this bodice." Mrs. Bella had been corrected several times about my name, to no avail. It was one detail too many to keep straight.

I dropped my arms and she slapped the tape across my chest, then pulled it around to the side. Her hands were dry and cold, and I felt goose bumps immediately spring up and spread, my snap reaction to any contact with Mrs. Bella. She was my mother's age but already had that thick, musty smell of old women and old clothes. She dragged a stepstool around to stand on and climbed up to inspect the tape.

"I do believe there must be tallness somewhere in your family, Mrs. McPhail," she said as she pulled the tape tighter, then let it drop. "Or maybe on your husband's side?"

"No," my mother said in the light voice she used whenever she wanted to encourage something to pass, "not really."

"It has to come from somewhere, right, Heaven?" She pulled a pincushion from her pocket and fastened the back of the dress, inserting one pin after the other.

"It's Haven," my mother said gently, trying to get me to look at her so that I could see her please-be-patient expression. I kept my eyes on the clock, on the second hand jumping around the face, and concentrated on time passing.

"Oh, right," Mrs. Bella said. "It's probably one of those—what do they call them, recessive genes? Only pops up every other generation or so."

My mother murmured softly, trying to move Mrs. Bella along. Ashley was walking around the room in her dress and bare feet while the assistant followed, fixing the train behind her. More employees were passing through now, with the clock nearing twelve-thirty. I could feel my face getting red. I felt gargantuan, my head almost brushing the ceiling, my arms dragging past Mrs. Bella to the pins on the floor. I had that image of pulling down the banners in the center court of the mall again, my hands clutching the fabric as it billowed before me. I imagined myself monsterlike, plodding like Godzilla through the aisles of Dillard's, searching out Mrs. Bella with her pin-filled mouth and recessive genes and hoisting her above my head in one fist, triumphant. I envisioned myself cutting a swath of destruction across the mall, across town itself, exacting revenge on everyone who stared at me or made the inevitable basketball jokes like I hadn't heard one ever before. My mind was soaring, filled with these images of chaos and revenge, when Mrs. Bella's voice cut through: "Okay, honey, the back's unpinned. With a little creative sewing I think we can get this dress to look right on you."

I looked down to see Ashley below me in her own dress, a vision of white fabric and tan skin, her face turned upward, hand clamping her headpiece. "Just don't grow for two weeks," she said to me, half-serious. "As a favor to me."

"Ashley!" my mother said, suddenly fed up with everyone. "Get out of the dress, Haven, and we'll go to lunch."

I went to change and slipped off the dress, careful not to stab myself with any of the hundreds of pins in the fabric. I put on my clothes and brought the dress out folded over my arm, handing it back to Mrs. Bella, who was now absorbed in sticking pins into Ashley, who deserved it. We left her standing there in all her white, as if waiting to be placed in the whipped-creamy center of a cake.

We had to eat at the mall, so we chose Sandwiches N' Such, which was a little place by Yogurt Paradise that sold fancy sandwiches and espresso and had little tables with white-and-red-checked tablecloths, like you were in Italy. We sat in the far corner, with the espresso machine sputtering behind us.

We didn't talk much at first. I ate my tuna fish on wheat and looked out at the crowd walking underneath the fluttering banners of the mall. My mother picked at her food, not eating so much as moving things from side to side. Something was bothering her.

"What's wrong?"

As soon as I asked she looked up at me, surprised. She'd never been comfortable with how easily I could read her, preferring to think she could still fool me by covering what was awful or scary with the sweep of her hand, the way she chased monsters out from under my bed when I was little.

"Well," she said, shifting in her chair, "I guess I just wanted a little time alone with you to take stock."

"Stock of what?" I concentrated on my food, picking around the mushy parts.

"Of us. You know, once the wedding is over and Ashley moves out, it's just going to be the two of us. Things will be different." She was working up to something. "I've thought a lot about this and it's best, I think, if I kept you apprised of what's happening. I don't want to make any major decisions without consulting you, Haven."

This tone, this jumble of important-sounding words, seemed too much like the kitchen-table talk we'd gotten the morning my father moved out. They'd come to us together, while I was eating my cereal, a united front announcing a split. That had been a long time ago, before my mother bought all her matching shorts-and-sandals sets and my father sprung new hair, a new wife, and a new beginning. But the feeling in my stomach was the same.

"Are you going to Europe?" I asked her.

"I don't know yet," she said. "I really want to go, but I'm worried about leaving you alone so soon after your sister moves out. And of course the fall, with you in school . . . the timing just isn't so good."

"I'd be okay," I said, watching a baby at the table next to us drooling juice all over himself. "If you want to go, you should go." I felt bad for not meaning this, even as I said it.

"Well, as I said, I haven't decided." She folded her napkin, over once and then again: a perfect square. "But there is something else I need to discuss with you."

"What?"

She sighed, placed the napkin in the dead even center of her plate, and said quickly, "I'm thinking about selling the house."

The moment she said it a picture of our house jumped into my head like a slide jerking up onto a screen during a school presentation. I saw my room and my mother's garden and the walk to the front door with day lilies blooming on either side. In my mind it was always summer, with the grass short and thick and the garden in full color, flowers waving in the breeze.

"Why?"

The hard part, the spitting out part, was done and now she relaxed. "Well, it's only going to be the two of us, and it would be cheaper if we moved somewhere smaller. We could find a nice apartment, probably, and save money. The house is really too big for just two people. We can't possibly fill it. Selling just seems like the logical choice."

"I don't want to move," I said a bit too loudly, and I was surprised at the sharp tone in my voice. "I can't believe you want to sell it."

"It's not a question of wanting to, necessarily. You don't know how expensive it is to keep it up, month after month. I'm only thinking of the best plan."

"I don't like the best plan." I didn't like any of it, suddenly, the changes and reorganizations and alterations to my life that were all in the control of other people and outside forces. I looked at my mother in her nice pink outfit and lipstick and Lydia-inspired frosted-and-cut hair and wanted to blame her for everything: the divorce and stupid Lewis and Ashley's wedding and even the height that set me to stooping and scrunching myself ever smaller, fighting nature's making my body betray me. But as I looked at her, at the concern in her face, I said none of this. I would push it back again, dig my heels into where I stood while the world shifted around me, what I'd considered givens suddenly lost to someone else's mistakes, miscalculations, or whims. A marriage, a sister, a house, each an elemental part of me, now gone.

"Haven, none of this is decided yet," my mother said, reaching across the table awkwardly to brush back my hair, her fingers smoothing my cheek. "Let's not get upset, okay? Maybe we can work something out."

"I'm sorry," I said, thinking of the tether again, pulling me back even as I strained to get away, to speak my mind. "I didn't mean to snap at you."

She smiled. "It's okay. I think we should all be allowed to yell at each other, at least once, before the wedding. It would probably do us all a lot of good."

Later, after we'd made small talk so that she could feel we'd ended on a good note, I sat alone at the table and stared out into the mall, putting off going to work. The Lakeview Models would make their first appearance the next weekend, kicking off the official start of mall season, each weekend an event or sales spectacular. It was a whole world, the mall, enclosed and safe, parameters neatly marked. Only Sumner seemed out of bounds, cruising in his golf cart wherever he pleased, keeping the peace and dodging the crowds. As I left I could see him over by the giant gumball machine, uniform on, looking official. He saw me and came over, leaving his cart safely parked by a row of ferns.

"You look upset," he observed, dropping into step beside me. His uniform cuffs rolled over his feet and hid his shoes.

"Well, it's been a long day," I said.

"What happened?" He waved at the owner of Shirts Etc., a round woman with jet black hair that had to be a wig. Her bangs were too neat, clipped straight across her forehead.

"I just had lunch with my mother."

"And how is she?"

"Fine. She's going to Europe." I was walking as slowly as I could, with the Little Feet sign looming up ahead.

The words were spelled out in shoes, just like on the boxes and the name tag in my pocket, which I would wait until the last possible second to put on.

"I love Europe," Sumner said, adjusting his glasses. "I went my sophomore year and had a grand time. Lots of pretty girls, if you don't mind underarm hair."

"Did you?"

"Did I what?"

"Mind underarm hair?"

He thought for a minute. "No. Not especially. But it depended on my mood and the extent of the hair itself. They have great chocolate in Europe, too. You should ask your mom to bring you some."

"I think we're going to move," I said, trying out the words for the first time. It felt strange. Again I saw my house, my room, the flowers. Maybe we'd end up in an apartment like Ashley's, all white paint and new carpet smell, with a splashing pool within earshot.

"Move where?" Now Sumner was waving at all the merchants. A few days on the job and he already knew everyone, exchanging inside jokes and winks as we passed each store. Again I felt that dizzying rush: of being with him, close to him, being taken along for the ride regardless of where he might be going; that hope that maybe somewhere in all this madness and confusion, he was the one who could understand me.

"My mother doesn't know," I said. "She just wants to sell the house."

"Oh." He nodded but didn't say anything right away. "That's tough."

"It's only 'cause of the divorce and Ashley moving

out," I said. "Just the two of us now, and all that. I don't know. Things have been so nuts lately."

"Yeah," he said. "When my parents got divorced it was really ugly. Everyone was fighting and I couldn't deal with it. I just packed up my car and took off. I didn't even know where I was going."

"How old were you?"

"I don't know . . . eighteen? It was the summer before I went to college. I just traveled around doing my thing, and by the time I got back everything had calmed down a little bit. And then I went off to college."

"I wish I could go somewhere," I said.

"I know what you mean. Sometimes, it just gets to be too much." Then he added, "Did you tell Ashley you saw me?"

"Yeah." I still had my mother on my mind, the house and the move and Europe all jumbled, and suddenly here Ashley was, the center of attention again. "I told her."

"What'd she say?"

I looked at him, wondering what was at stake here, then said, "She didn't say much. She's got a lot on her mind now."

"Oh, yeah." He shrugged it off. "Well, sure. I just wondered if she remembered me, you know. If she ran screaming from the room at the mention of my name."

"Nothing that dramatic," I said. "She just . . . she said to say hello if I saw you again."

"Really?" He was surprised. "Wow."

"I mean, it was casual and all," I said quickly, worried that this little lie might carry more weight than I meant it to. I couldn't tell him how she'd hardly blinked, hanging over the porch with her hair shielding her face. How it had barely jarred her mind from the wedding and Lewis and even the smallest thought she might have been thinking. No one wants to be inconsequential.

"Oh, I know," he said. "I just wondered if she even remembered me."

"She does," I said as we came up on Little Feet, with sneakers bobbing on fishing line in the window and paper fish I'd made myself stuck to the wall behind them. "You're not so forgettable."

"Yeah, well. I don't know about that." He stopped at the door to the store, sweeping his arm. "And here we are."

"Yeah." I looked in to see my manager folding socks. When he saw me he took a not so subtle look at the clock, craning his long, rubbery neck. I hated my job. "You know you could always drop in at Dillard's and see her. She works at the Vive cosmetics counter."

He smiled. "I don't think that's such a great idea. There's no telling what might happen when she saw me."

My manager was watching me, folding sock over sock. "You could at least say hello. I mean, it wasn't like you ever did anything to *her*."

Sumner looked up. He stared at me as if my face was changing before him, and then said slowly, "Well, no. I guess not. Look, I better go, Haven. I've got to get back to work."

"Me too." I pulled out my name tag and put it on, fastening the clip. "Think about it, Sumner. It's not like she ever hated you." I didn't know why this was so important to me; maybe I thought he could bring back the Ashley I liked so much, the one who liked me. Maybe Sumner's magic could work on both of us again.

He started to back away, hands in his pockets. He looked smaller to me now, lost in the green of his uniform. "Yeah. I'll see you later."

I stood there and watched him walk away, still stalling for time while the second hand of the store clock jumped closer and closer to two o'clock. The mall was noisy and busy now, with people and voices and colors all jumbled together, another Saturday of shopping and families and bright red plastic Lakewood Mall bags. Still I kept my eye on Sumner as he waded through the throngs past the potted plants and swaying banners overhead. He'd been where I was, once; he understood. I watched him go until he was lost to me, another green in a sea of multicolors, shifting.

Chapter Eight

In the time that she'd been home, Casey had managed not only to be grounded for smoking, but also to get caught making hour-long interstate calls to Pennsylvania, drinking a beer behind the garden shed during a family barbecue, and disappearing for an entire day. Mrs. Melvin was exhausted and sick of Casey's face, so she granted her a leave of two hours to come to see me, provided she called in every half hour and got home by six. She arrived two seconds after inviting herself over, breathless.

"My mom wants to kill me," she said as we set out

for a walk around the neighborhood and a chance to talk in private. "I heard her and my dad discussing my situation last night, on the back porch."

"And she said she wanted to kill you?"

"No, she said she was beginning to think the only solution was to lock me in my room." She pushed a mass of orange curls out of her face. "But then she lets me out today. I think she's up to something."

"You're paranoid," I told her.

"Last night when I called Rick he said he was getting it from his parents, too. He can't call for a while." She sighed, crossing her arms against her shirt, a long white polo ten sizes too big. I wondered if Rick had any clothes of his own left. I imagined him leaving 4-H camp naked, with Casey packing up everything he owned as a souvenir.

"It's only till Thanksgiving," I said, trying to be helpful. It hadn't happened to me yet, this swirling mass of emotions that made all the women around me behave so erratically.

"Thanksgiving is forever away," she whined as we took the corner and headed down the street parallel to our own. "I'm going nuts here and it's been less than a week. I've got to find some way to get up there."

"Get up where?"

She rolled her eyes. "Pennsylvania. God, Haven, aren't you paying attention?"

"Not when you start talking like a crazy person. You don't even drive yet."

"I will, in two and a half weeks." With the wedding so close, I'd forgotten her birthday was coming up. "Dad's been taking me out every night to drive around and I know they're going to give me my grandmother's Delta 88. They think it's a secret and I don't know why it's in the garage, but I know."

"Even if you are about to get your license," I said as a mass of kids on bikes passed us, all of them in helmets and knee pads, little punks terrorizing the neighborhood, "they'd never let you take off to Pennsylvania."

"Of course they wouldn't let me." She said this matter-of-factly, as if I was slow and just not getting it. Since Casey had gone wild at 4-H camp, it seemed like we had less and less in common. "But that doesn't mean I can't go. I just slip out, see, in the middle of the night, and call them the next morning when I'm in, like, Maryland. By then they're just so crazed with worry they're just happy I'm alive, so they let me go on. Then I come back and get punished forever but it's worth it because I get to be with Rick."

I looked at her. "That will never work."

She stuck out her bottom lip, something she'd gotten good at in the last week, and said, "Yes it will."

"Oh, like Rick's parents wouldn't send you home the second you showed up. They're not going to let you just hang out while your parents are sitting around here waiting for you to get home so they can kill you."

She was staring at the sidewalk as I said this, making a point of not looking at me. After a minute she said in a tight voice, "You don't understand, Haven. You couldn't. You've never been in love."

"Oh please," I said, suddenly fed up. I was sick of hearing about Rick and Pennsylvania and camp stories.

I couldn't talk to anyone anymore. Sumner seemed like the only one who listened at all, the only one who asked for nothing and took nothing from me.

"You know what your problem is," Casey began, her hand poised to shake at me, but then she stopped dead, sucking in her breath. She grabbed my shirt, tugging, and pointed across one of the yards.

It was Gwendolyn Rogers. Or at least the back of Gwendolyn Rogers. Her hair was pulled up in a high ponytail and she was wearing a black string bikini top, standing there in the backyard all by herself. She had her hands on her hips and was staring off across the yard, over the wall and into the next yard. She was standing very, very still.

I heard a woman's voice, suddenly, wafting out from the open downstairs windows of the house. "Gwendolyn? Gwennie, are you down here? Gwendolyn?" It was a mother's voice.

Gwendolyn didn't move, so still and tall, so much like the trees around her. She was enormous, and for the first time in so long I felt small, no bigger than a minute.

Casey was still pulling on my shirt, pointing like I hadn't seen anything and saying, "That's her, God, Haven, *look*."

I was looking. And listening to Mrs. Rogers's voice as it moved past one window after another, growing louder, then fading. Finally she came out on the back porch, where we could only see the top of her head over the wall, being that she was normal sized. Softly, she said, "Gwendolyn?" The top of her head moved across the yard, until it was flush with the middle of Gwendo-lyn's spine. I saw a hand come up, tiny, and take one of the long, thin arms. "Let's go in, honey, okay? Maybe you should lie down for a little while."

Her voice was very clear and soft, the kind you hear at your bedside when you're sick and throwing up and your mother brings cold compresses and ginger ale and oyster crackers. Mrs. Rogers rubbed her hand up and down Gwendolyn's arm, talking now in a low voice that I couldn't make out; but Gwendolyn didn't move a mus-cle. Finally, Gwendolyn turned. I saw her face then, the same one we'd seen on all those magazine covers and on MTV. But it wasn't the same: it wasn't bronzed, with pink lips and lashes a mile long; no hair blowing back in the wind, framing her face; no diamonds flashing out of the wild blue of her eyes. Instead, I saw just a tall girl with a blank, plain expression, thin and angular and lost. Her cheeks were hollow and her mouth small, not luscious, more like a slit drawn hastily with a marker or a child's crayon. I don't know if she saw us. She was looking our way, her eyes on us, but there was no way of telling what she saw. It could have been us or the trees behind us or maybe another place or faces of other people. She only looked at us for a few moments, with that haunted, gaunt expression before her mother prodded her along and she ducked into the doorway, vanishing.

"Did you see her?" Casey was standing in their yard now, craning her head to get a look inside. "God, can you believe it? She looks horrible."

"We should go," I said, now aware that they could

be in any of those windows, watching us. It seemed like too small a house to hold someone so big, like a doll's house with tiny plates and newspapers.

I practically had to drag Casey down the sidewalk. She was sure Gwendolyn was going to make another appearance, or burst out the door for another hysterical walk through the neighborhood.

"Come on," I said, then gave up trying to move her forcibly and just took off myself, much the way I always did when she was doing something that could get us both in trouble.

She came along, complaining all the way. "If we'd stayed, she might have come out and talked to us. She's probably lonely."

"She doesn't even know us," I said as we turned back onto our street. Mrs. Melvin's flag, emblazoned with a strawberry, flapped in the breeze a few houses down. The bike gang passed again, this time in the street, yelling and shooting us the finger. They were all elementary school kids.

"She knows we feel her pain," said Casey, who suddenly had personal insight into this herself. "I know what it feels like."

"You do not," I said as we came up to the Melvins' house. "All you know is loving some dumb guy in Pennsylvania."

"Love is love is love," Casey said, stubborn. "We women know."

We were passing her house anyway, so Casey stopped for the first half-hour check. Mrs. Melvin was in the kitchen, making some kind of fancy meal that required the peeling of an eggplant. Baby Ronald was at the kitchen table eating baloney slices and playing with his Star Trek action figures.

"Just to let you know I haven't run off to Pennsylvania," Casey said, heading straight to the fridge. The room smelled like burnt rice. I could hear Charlie Baker, news anchorman, talking about national affairs from the small TV that sat on the counter by the bananas.

"Not funny." Mrs. Melvin put down the eggplant, which was a sickly brown color without its purple skin. "Don't forget we have dinner at six-fifteen. It's family night."

Casey pulled out two cans of Diet Pepsi and made a face at me. "God, how much time do I have to spend with you guys, anyway?"

Mrs. Melvin went back to the eggplant, her mouth in that tight little line that meant she was cranky. "I'm not in the mood to answer that question."

"Hey, baby Ronald," I said, pulling out a chair and sitting down across from him.

He scowled, wrinkling his nose. Freckles folded in, then out. "Shut up."

"Ronald," Mrs. Melvin snapped. "That's rude."

"I'm not a baby," he protested.

"Yes you are," Casey said.

"Well, you're in trouble," Ronald said indignantly, slapping a piece of baloney on the table and marching a Klingon across it.

"And you're stupid," Casey said. "So stuff it."

"Casey," Mrs. Melvin said in a tired voice, "please."

I turned my attention back to the TV, where I could

see the entire Action News Team paired off at their two sets of desks. Charlie Baker and Tess Phillips on one side, grimly shuffling papers as we came back from a commercial; and off to the other, my father and Lorna, smiling and whispering to each other. My father had even more hair than the last time I'd seen him. He'd never had that much, even when I was little. Lorna was beside him, hands crossed on the desk in front of her.

"And now for the weather, let's check in with Lorna Queen's Weather Scene," Charlie Baker boomed in his big voice while the camera panned across to Lorna's smiling face. She stood up, today in a hot-pink miniskirt and jacket, and strolled over to the weather map.

"Thanks, Charlie. Today was gorgeous, right, folks? I wish I could tell you there was more of the same coming, but we haven't quite gotten over the heat yet. Let's take a look at the national map. You'll see that a front is moving over the mid-Atlantic states, producing some heavy showers. . . ."

I tuned Lorna out, instead watching her gesture her way across the fifty states, sweeping her arm over the map as if she could create showers or drought on a whim. I wondered if anyone ever really listened to her at all.

Now she was standing in front of the Five Day Forecast. ". . . right up until Tuesday, but I've got to say I can't promise much for Wednesday through Friday. Look for some high cloud cover, the normal afternoon thunderstorm, and of course high temperatures and Charlie's favorite, lots of humidity. Right, Charlie?"

The camera panned back to Charlie, who was caught playing with his pencil and mumbled something quickly before it zoomed back to Lorna. Now she was standing in front of a video of a bunch of children chasing bunny rabbits across the grass. "And finally, I just wanted to thank all the kids at the Little Ones day-care center, where I went today to do a Weather Scene Class. We talked about rain and snow and had some fun with the bunnies they have there, as you can see. Great kids." She waved at the camera. "A special hello to all of them. Thanks for having me!"

"Good God," Casey said dramatically, rolling her eyes.

"Casey," Mrs. Melvin said, throwing the peeler in the sink.

"I'm just saying."

Lorna was done waving now and took her seat next to my father again. Charlie Baker shuffled his papers around, looking official, and then said, "Thanks, Lorna. I'm looking forward to that humidity you promised me."

"A little late to get in on that joke," Casey said. "He's such a cheeseball."

Tess Phillips leaned across Charlie Baker, smiling her newswoman smile. "And I understand you have a special report of your own over there, Lorna."

Lorna blushed, pinkly, and I got that sinking feeling in my stomach again. "Well, yes, both Mac and I do. Right, honey?"

"That's right," my father said. He seemed bigger with all that hair.

"We're expecting!" Lorna squealed. "I'm due in March!"

On the television, in the Action News newsroom, there was an explosion of congratulations, slapping of backs, and general good spirits. In the Melvins' kitchen it was too quiet and everyone was suddenly looking at me.

"Expecting?" Casey said. "How is that possible? The wedding was less than a month ago; there's no way she could already be pregnant. Unless it happened *before*, but . . ."

"Casey," Mrs. Melvin said in a low voice. "Hush."

I stared at my father on the screen, watching him smile proudly at the viewing public before they cut to a commercial. Suddenly I wanted to go home.

"God, Haven. Why didn't you tell me?" Casey was standing behind me now, her hand on the back of my chair.

"Look, I better get going." I kept my eyes on the commercial for satellite dishes. Baby Ronald stomped his figures across the table, staging a war by the sugar bowl.

"I'll walk you," Casey said.

"No," I said quickly. "That's all right. I'll call you later."

"You okay?"

I could feel Mrs. Melvin, mouth of the neighborhood, watching me and taking notes for the next neighborhood gossip session. "Fine. I just forgot I had to be home."

"Okay, well, call me." She walked me to the door, holding it open as I stepped out onto the patio. "Seriously. I'm like a prisoner here." Mrs. Melvin still had her eyes on me, eggplant in her hand.

"I'll call." I started down the driveway, sucking in the thick, humid air of late summer, heavy in my lungs.

It was late afternoon and all the kids were out, bike punks and Big Wheels, and mothers with strollers grouped on the corner, no doubt passing the latest about nervous breakdowns and tuna casseroles and failing marriages, the goods on the neighborhood. I made it to the end of the driveway and hit the sidewalk, feeling each step in my shins as if by the sheer force of pounding my feet on the ground I could force the world out from under me.

As I walked I kept seeing my father in my mind, with his hair and that smile, proud and bursting, father-to-be. Lorna Queen with her little ears and blond hair. A baby with my father's round face and my last name. My father's new life was progressing as planned, one neat step at a time. And I felt it, again, that same feeling I got whenever another change or shift in my life was announced to me—selling the house, Ashley's tantrums, now the baby—that need to dig in my heels and prepare myself for the *next* shock and its aftermath. I was tired of hanging on, taking the torn pieces to make something whole with them.

I stopped suddenly, breathless, unsure of where I was. The houses in my neighborhood all looked the same, one floor plan reversed and then back again. More kids on bikes, more mothers on corners, flags with watermelon and sunshine designs hanging from front porches. I could have lived in any of these houses. Any of these families could have been mine, once.

The tight, throbbing feeling in my throat made me want to start sobbing, to break down, right there on an unfamiliar corner in front of a house just like my own.

Everything seemed so out of control, as if even running the streets wouldn't save me. I wondered if this was how Gwendolyn felt running wild at night, this lost, loose feeling that no consequence could be so harmful as the sense of staying where you were, or of being who you are. I wanted to be somewhere else, out of the range of my mother's voice and ears, of Ashley's pouty looks, of the News Channel 5 viewing area. Someplace where the sight of me sobbing would tie me to no one and no one to me.

I was going to let it happen, let the tears come and the sobs rise up from my chest. I imagined crying until I was exhausted, dry, finally letting it all go.

And then I heard that *blub-blub-blub* puttering around the corner where I stood. Sumner was behind the wheel, so busy adjusting the stereo that he didn't even see me at first. Just as I thought to call his name he glanced over his shoulder.

He backed up beside me, smoothly aligning with the curb. The passenger seat was filled with books, heavy black volumes with gold monograms. "Hey, Haven. What's going on?"

Even as he spoke I was doing it, breathing in and clearing my head, swallowing until the lump in my throat disappeared. Digging my heels in again, regulating myself. "Nothing," I said.

"Need a ride?" He started pushing books into the back.

"Sure." I climbed in and we were off, puttering along the short distance to my house, passing the Rogerses', familiar territory. Sumner pulled off his tie and reached across me to stuff it in the glove compartment.

"So," he said after a while. "What's wrong?"

"Nothing," I said. "It's just . . . my father and his new wife are going to have a baby."

"A baby?"

"Yeah. They just got married."

He smiled. "Wow. They didn't waste any time, huh?"

"I guess not," I said. "I mean, it's like this just makes it official. My father has completely begun his life over." We passed the Melvins', where baby Ronald was playing on the steps.

"Well, maybe he is. And that sucks. But it doesn't mean he's forgetting you or anything," he said, tapping his fingers against the steering wheel. "It'll work out, Haven. This is the worst of it."

I knew he was probably right. It seemed like every time I saw Sumner lately I was reacting to a crisis. And every time, he said the one thing, the *right* thing, that no one else could say.

"So," I asked him, "what are you doing around these parts?"

"Selling encyclopedias. It's a new job. My first day, actually."

"Did you sell any?"

"No, but three people invited me in for soda. One of them was really old, too old for encyclopedias, but we looked at all her photo albums and talked about the war."

"I didn't think you could ever be too old for encyclopedias," I said.

"Maybe not," he said, "but according to my marketing manual eighty-five-year-old widows with ten cats and a houseful of dusty antiques are not writing a lot of term papers. Heard some great war stories, though. There's nothing like a good war story."

He slowed down; we were coming to my house. Ashley was walking up the front steps, still in her work clothes. She wore that damn lab coat everywhere.

We pulled up to the curb just as she got to the door, but she was digging for her keys and didn't notice us. She didn't remember the sound of the car the way I did. I wondered how she could ever have forgotten, but Ashley was always good at that.

We watched her fumbling in her purse, which was balanced against her knee. She brushed her hair impatiently out of her face, then tucked it behind her ear. Under her lab coat she had on a red dress that showed off her tan and wore black sandals over her tiny little feet. I thought again of her Barbie adolescence and how I'd envied her, and I looked at Sumner, at the expression I couldn't read on his face. I wondered how she looked to him, if she was older or fatter or just the same as that last time he saw her on the porch, when she put a door between him and herself. Finally she found her keys, opened the door, and kicked it shut behind her, rattling the glass. I still hadn't gotten out of the car.

"Do you want to come in?" I asked him.

"Oh no," he said. "I have to get to work."

"At the mall?"

"No." He shifted in his seat, reaching behind to pull out a stack of records: Lawrence Welk, Jimmy Dorsey, the Andrews Sisters. "I'm getting fifty bucks to dance with old women at the senior center. They're having a nostalgia dance but they're short on men. I'm not supposed to tell them I'm getting paid, though. It would ruin the spirit of it all."

"You dance?"

He sighed. "Sure. My mother thought she was Ginger Rogers. Didn't Ashley tell you? I taught her every dance she knows."

"I didn't even know Ashley could dance."

"You should see her waltz," he said, putting the records back behind the seat. "She's incredible. Of course, she always wanted to lead. She's not much of a follower, you know."

"I know." I wondered if Ashley was looking out at us. "You sure you don't want to come in? My mom would love to see you."

"Nah," he said, shaking his head. "Not now. I gotta go."

I got out of the car, shutting the door behind me. "Thanks for the ride."

"Well, you didn't have far to go."

"No. But it was nice anyway."

" 'Bye, Haven. Hang in there." He started the engine and the blubbing built to a noisy peak before leveling off steady. I stood on the curb, watching him drive away, and just as he turned the corner I thought of my father and Lorna again, and the baby with its tiny ears. Even Sumner and his jobs and jokes couldn't make some things go away.

Chapter Nine

⤳

That *weekend was* the official premiere of the Lakeview Models in the annual Back to School Fall Preview Fashion Show. The name had been changed, however, to the Back to School Fall Preview Fashion Show Featuring a Special Appearance by Former Lakeview Model Gwendolyn Rogers; someone had gone around with a magic marker and added on to all the signs. I wondered how Gwendolyn was feeling, if she was still out staring in her backyard or pacing the neighborhood in the wee hours of the morning, or if she even cared about the Lakeview Models at all, in the midst of her rumored nervous breakdown. I'd been thinking about Gwendolyn Rogers a lot lately as I sat awake in my own bed, staring at the ceiling and wondering what could happen next. Sometimes I even listened for the sound of her feet on the pavement outside, the rustle of her passing, the shallow breaths I imagined of someone gone wild. I was sure I'd heard her, at least once.

The whole town turned out for the Fall Fashion Preview that Saturday; but since most people were not interested in buying children's shoes, Marlene and I took turns walking down to the main stage and reporting back on the activity. In the early part of the morning, there was a great racket of chairs being set up and people shouting to each other. Around noon, the models arrived and began to get ready in the store that had been Holland Farms Cheeses and Gifts until it had just recently gone out of business. Now it had a sign in the front window that read Model Prep Area, with the words Authorized Persons Only, Please written in firm little letters beneath it. They were in there, cooing and giggling. You could hear them from outside, where all the younger girls and those who hadn't made it were grouped, trying to catch a glimpse of Gwendolyn or the models or anyone even slightly related to the whole process. And of course Sumner was there in his uniform, carrying a clipboard and looking official.

I was off for the day at one-thirty because I had the early shift, so I got to see the entire production. Casey and I met by the stage and took seats in the back, behind the mothers of the models and the screaming children that fill the mall every day and all the people with cameras out to get a good shot of Gwendolyn Rogers, Supermodel.

"I can't tell you how I've been dying to get out of the house," Casey said as we sat down. She was in another big shirt, this time an old rugby with worn elbows. "My mother is driving me nuts. She won't let me near the phone or out the door without giving me the third degree, and I know she's been in my room." I was watching the stage as she spoke, which now had two white partitions covering the big leaves I'd seen a few weeks ago.

"You can't tell," I said.

"Yes I can, because I set traps for her." She crossed her arms against her chest, triumphant. "I left a hair shut in my dresser drawer and in the latch of the box I keep all my important stuff in, and when I checked after coming home the other day they were both gone."

I looked at her. "Hairs?"

"I saw it in a movie." She flipped her hair and rolled her eyes, a combination of moves she'd picked up at camp along with all her other bad habits. "It's drastic, I know, but something had to be done."

"But she still went through your stuff," I told her. "It's not stopping her, it's just proving the fact."

"Right. And I have ammunition when I accuse her of invading my privacy. I'll tell her I can prove it and then watch her squirm." She sighed. "It'll be ugly, but like I said, there's no love in war."

"It's not really a war, Casey."

"It's close to it. You know Rick's parents won't even

let him talk to me anymore? Every time I call they say he's busy or at practice or something. I haven't talked to him in a week."

"He hasn't called you?"

"He probably has and my parents don't tell me. I swear to it, Haven, they want me miserable. They hate Rick and they haven't even met him." Behind us some baby started howling.

It was amazing what a summer could do. Before camp my best friend, Casey Melvin, was a short, pudgy redhead who hung back at introductions, couldn't look a boy in the eye, and spent every Sunday afternoon taking tap-dancing lessons with her mother. Now she was at war with her parents, angry at the world in general, and more than a little bit paranoid. I wondered if the summer had changed me, if with one look the world could see a difference.

"Ladies and gentlemen, on behalf of the Lakeview Mall I would like to welcome you to the annual Fall Fashion Preview!" Everyone looked around for the source, since in years before, the show had relied on a woman with a loud voice to yell the commentary from side stage. The voice came from a speaker mounted on a plant right behind us: the Lakeview Mall had gone high tech. "And to begin our festivities, we have a very special guest. Please give a big welcome to our very own former Lakeview Mall Model and hometown girl, Gwendolyn Rogers!"

Now everyone looked at the stage, apparently think-ing Gwendolyn would suddenly pop out of nowhere like the voice had, and there she was, tall and haunting, walking slowly up the center aisle as heads turned, row by row.

She looked terrible, her face gaunt, the famous Gwendolyn lips that pursed out from all those magazine pages now slack and thin, her hair lying flat on her head, even a bit stringy. She was wearing a short skirt and a silk tank top that was wrinkled, with sandals that scraped against the floor with each step she took. But it was the walk that was the strangest, after seeing her striding down runway after runway in music videos and on television, her head held high and hips swaying to the music, eye on the camera, as if she knew how you envied her. Now she was tentative, taking light steps and holding herself tight even though she had the whole enormous aisle to spread out in. We were all applauding because we had to, but she seemed lost and uncomfortable, and when she reached the bottom stair that led to the stage I felt myself let loose a breath, relieved she had made it. The applause died out as Gwendolyn climbed the steps. The official Lakeview Mall greeter was waiting with her clipboard. She had been beaming, but suddenly her smile died and she squinted at Gwendolyn uncertainly, as if expecting her to collapse on the spot.

The emcee shook her hand and led her to the podium. Gwendolyn, towering above her, stood behind the microphone and looked out at us with the same dim, lost look that I'd seen the other day. She cleared her throat once and then jumped a bit as the sound echoed from one speaker to another to another. I wondered if she was sedated.

"It's spooky," Casey whispered to me, and I nodded.

A woman in front of me said loudly, "She looks like she's on drugs or something. Damn good example to set for the kids here. She shouldn't even be on the stage."

"Hush," her friend said.

"I'm just saying," the woman replied, shifting in her chair. "And look at that hair."

We were all looking.

The emcee next to Gwendolyn stood on tiptoe and whispered something in her ear, but Gwendolyn's face never changed. She cleared her throat again, and we waited.

"Thank you for having me," she began slowly, and we all relaxed a bit. Things were going to be okay. "It's a real treat to be here overseeing a new generation of Lakeview Models."

The emcee began applauding, looking nervous, so we all joined in. Gwendolyn was still staring at the back of the mall.

The silence had gone on too long now. I wished for words to come from her mouth, any sound that might get her through this. Her hands were gripping the sides of the podium, the tips of her fingers white from the strain. It was as if the Gwendolyn we all knew and expected had been left behind on those glossy magazine pages—or had never existed at all. She opened her mouth, took in a breath; I closed my eyes until I heard her voice echo around me.

"So without further ado, let's begin this year's show." Her voice was flat, even, and as the woman ushered her off the stage to her seat of honor in the front row,

Gwendolyn ran her fingers over her long, stringy hair, obscuring her face as she passed by. Once seated, her head stuck up above the crowd, and I watched as the people behind her, no longer charmed, grumbled and rearranged themselves.

Suddenly there was a burst of music, so loud that a woman behind me actually shrieked. It was disco, a fast beat and lots of technological-sounding blips and beeps along with the occasional loud panting of a woman's voice. We all stared up at the stage, waiting for something while the music pounded on behind us. Then, the partitions slowly parted (with the help of Sumner and some other guy in a uniform, who tried hard to stay out of sight), revealing the leaves I'd seen before. Now, however, there were lights spinning across them, blue and green and red and yellow, catching bits of glitter that I hadn't noticed until now. It was all a bit overwhelming, a definite change from the show of last year, which consisted of one lone ficus tree that the models walked by, posed around, and then pulled to the edge of the stage for the big finale, where they threw its leaves on the audience to symbolize fall. That fashion show had been the most innovative, until this year.

Suddenly, the music stopped, and the lights fell steady on the leaves, each a different color. The disembodied voice came again. "Ladies and gentlemen, please join the Lakeview Mall Models as we journey into fall. A fall of expectations . . . of new ideas . . . and of potential. Come, come with us . . ."

"Oh, for Christ's sake," someone behind us said loudly.

". . . to a world of color and style, of tweed and tartan, of reality and imagination. Close your eyes and feel the cool air, the sharp colors of the leaves, and the dreams of winter. Come, come, and journey with us . . . into the Fall of Fashion."

The lights started swirling again, the music came on full blast, and suddenly the models began to walk up on stage, each of them smiling big toothy smiles and vamping like nobody's business. The first was a girl in a beret who flounced out on the runway, tossed her hat in the air Mary Tyler Moore style, and just let it fall on some woman in the second row who looked like she wasn't quite sure whether to throw it back or keep it. Beret girl was replaced by a girl in a long tweed jacket who took it off and dragged it dramatically down the runway with such abandon that someone behind me began to speculate about the cost of dry-cleaning it. The next girl clomped down the runway in torn jeans and combat boots, tossing her hair and gyrating suggestively, grinning out at us. A group of older women, probably remembering the tame ficus-tree show of the previous year, made a big fuss of leaving in disgust.

It only got worse. The music switched to just a woman moaning, over and over again, and one girl actually came out in hip-length black leather boots, which sent a flurry of exclamations down the crowd and another set of people packing up and leaving. The models were oblivious, most of them making a point of playing specifically to Gwendolyn Rogers as if to prove they were just like her, real *models*. Gwendolyn's head, however, bowed forward, as if even watching was too much for her.

For the grand finale, which was always a showcase of evening wear for Christmas balls and dances, the models came out in tight black dresses and spike heels, with their hair pulled straight back and lips bright red, the rest of their faces white and pale as if they were very sick. They stopped to pose, waiting for the applause to thunder down upon them.

We applauded, those of us who were left, and watched as the director of the show, a young guy in a purple suit with a walkie-talkie in his hand, came up for his bow. I wondered if he realized that the entire board of the Lakeview Mall was probably waiting for him offstage, ready to wring his neck. When they brought Gwendolyn back up to address the models there weren't that many people left in the audience, which was probably a good thing.

They stuck Gwendolyn in the middle and the models giggled and panted and shuffled around to get closer, their lips red and bright. As the photographer took pictures, she was pale in the center, towering above them all with their black dresses and pulled-back hair, their pale skin and scary Halloween lips, looking down at them as they crowded in around her. And then, just as they were all saying cheese once more, smiling for the camera on their big day, Gwendolyn Rogers burst into tears.

No one knew how to react at first; she was just suddenly crying, tears running down her face as she stood there, surrounded by these girls who wanted to be just like her. The models moved away, uncertain, as if by proximity they could catch whatever she had, as if sorrow was infectious. No one did anything to help her.

Then I saw Mrs. Rogers; she was coming up the center aisle, her purse clutched against her hip, almost running but trying to look calm. She climbed the stairs and came up behind Gwendolyn, who was making little whimpering sounds that embarrassed me for her. I didn't even watch, focusing instead on a wad of gum that was stuck on the floor. I heard them passing: Mrs. Rogers's voice soothing and calm, saying, "All you need is rest, honey," and Gwendolyn's jarred and ragged, replying, "It's so awful, they just don't know how awful it is, those poor girls."

Casey watched them, attentive, then tapped my shoulder. "Let's get out of here."

I nodded and followed her, and we wove our way down the middle aisle, which was now suddenly crowded with models' mothers (most of whom were biting their lips and looking irritated), a few men in suits with strained looks (I was sure they had to be the contingent of mall management), and a bunch of women talking in hushed voices about how shocking it all was. I lost Casey in the blur of perfume and general mayhem, then found her waiting for me by a planter full of ferns.

"Can you believe that?" she asked me as we started walking down in the direction of Little Feet. "A total breakdown, right in the middle of the Fall Fashion Preview. She has to have totally lost it. She's nuts."

"God, Casey," I said, suddenly nervous that Gwendolyn was still in earshot. "She's sick."

"She's nuts, Haven," she said with authority, pulling out a pack of gum and offering me a piece. "Beautiful and nuts. What a combination."

We were coming up on Sumner now, who was busy talking with some woman who had a baby attached to her hip and a toddler linked to her wrist by one of those baby leashes. The kid was straining on it, yanking towards the toy store, but kept getting jerked back, losing his balance, and crashing to the floor. The mother was too busy fussing at Sumner to even notice.

"I'm not the kind of person who usually complains," she was saying as we got within earshot. "But I really feel like that was just a disgusting display and completely unnecessary. Those aren't the kind of clothes a girl would wear back to school. What happened to plaid jumpers? To tights and slacks? To those nice sweaters with the reindeer prints on them?"

"I don't know, ma'am," Sumner said in a deep voice. "I can't really say."

"Well, it just upsets me." She yanked on the leash, plopping the toddler, who had managed to make some headway, back to the floor again. "I feel like it just sends the wrong message, you know? I don't associate gyrating with homework, myself, and I don't think any other mother who spends money at this mall does, either."

"I completely understand," Sumner said, and then saw me and smiled. "I would suggest contacting mall management. I'm sure they'd be very concerned about what you're saying. Here's the number right here, or if you'd like to write a letter—"

"Yes, a letter might be better," she said. "It's always better to put it in writing, isn't it?"

"It is indeed." Sumner wrote something on a card and handed it to her. "That's the man to address, right there. In case you decide to call, he's not in on Tuesdays."

"Thank you." She put the card in her fanny pack and leaned over the toddler, who was now sitting on the floor eating a dirty candy wrapper. We watched as she got him to his feet, adjusted the baby to her other hip, and they walked off down the mall together, the leash hanging between them.

"Hey," Sumner said, coming over to us, "quite a show, huh?"

Casey was just staring at him, with a sudden sparkle in her eye that I didn't like, so I said, "Sumner, this is Casey. Casey, this is Sumner. He's an old—"

"Family friend," Sumner put in. "I like to think I'm more than just one among the crowd of Ashley's ex-boyfriends. I want to believe I made my mark."

"You did," I said. He had to know how important he was. "You were the best of all of them."

He laughed. "I wouldn't say that."

"How old are you?" Casey asked him, her head cocked to the side like she was Nancy Drew solving a mystery.

"Twenty-one," Sumner said, glancing down at his uniform. "And it shows, doesn't it?"

"Not really," Casey said, and her voice was different,

long and drawling. And I didn't like the way she was standing, either, all cutesy in her big shirt and cutoffs, smiling at Sumner like he was some guy at camp.

"Well, we better go," I said, wanting to move on. Suddenly I wasn't so sure I wanted to share Sumner with Casey, who saw boys only as people to take shirts from and pine for. I wasn't sure I wanted to share him with anyone. "I've got to get home."

"You do not," Casey said, using that same voice on me now, high and flirty. "God, Haven's always having to go home and do something, isn't she? She's such a good girl."

I looked at her. "I am not."

"Oh Gawd," she said, "honestly. Anyone looks bad compared to you, Little Miss Do Whatever Anyone Wants You To."

Sumner looked at me, then said, "Ah, but you do not know Haven as I do."

"I've known her all my life," Casey said, now smacking her gum, which she thought made her look cool (she was wrong), "and I know."

"She's a wild one," he said, grinning at me, making it up on the spot. I loved it, every bit. "Maybe sometime she'll tell you about it."

Casey looked at me, still smacking. "You must have the wrong girl, Sumner."

"Nope. That's her," he said, pointing at me as he turned to walk away. "I know. Take it easy, Haven. Nice to meet you."

"You too," Casey called after him, waggling her fingers. She waited for him to get lost in the crowd and then said, "Why didn't you tell me about him? He's so cute."

"He's just Sumner," I said. "He dated Ashley forever."

"Well, he's fine as hell," she said, using another expression she'd picked up at camp. "All this time you're after some guy at the mall and you didn't even tell me."

"It's not like that," I said.

"Why not? You should be after him, big time. He seems to like you already. Can you imagine, you dating a college boy? That would be so cool!"

"He's my friend," I said, amazed that Casey could take Sumner away from me and twist him into something else, something almost dirty. That wasn't what he was to me.

"Whatever," she said, still smacking her gum. "If it was me, I'd be after him."

"You don't understand," I said quietly, not wanting to talk about it anymore. Me and Sumner—that was ridiculous. He was Ashley's old boyfriend, for godsakes. And Casey didn't understand because she couldn't. She hadn't seen her whole life change in the last few years, hadn't had everything taken away. His reappearing was proof that the time I looked back to had actually happened. This summer, Sumner was just what I needed.

Chapter Ten

The wedding countdown, suddenly reduced to single digits, continued. With eight days to go to The Big Day, Ashley had her bachelorette party, which allowed her a full week to recover from the night of drinking, giggling, and general secret activity that her friends had been planning since the engagement. I'd overheard my mother saying something to Lydia Catrell about strippers and tequila, but since I was underage I went along for dinner and then was dropped off unceremoniously on my front lawn while the rest of the group sped off to places unknown. I watched television until late and fell asleep on the couch, remote still in my hand, then woke up when I heard scratching at the front door. The doorbell rang, a few times, among an explosion of giggling, the slamming of car doors, and a beeping horn. I opened the front door and found my sister splayed out on the porch, missing a shoe, wearing what appeared to be underwear around her neck, and mumbling.

"Ashley?" I wasn't quite sure what to do. "Are you okay?"

"Mmmhpgh." She rolled over so that she was flat on her back; her face was red. "Haven."

I leaned over her, smelled her breath, and then took a few steps back. Across the street, Duckdog started barking. "Yes?"

"Help me inside." She reached up, waving her arm at me crookedly. I grabbed it and pulled her over the threshold, bumping her head on the door. "Ouch," she whined. "That hurts."

"Sorry." We were inside now, so I dropped her arm and kicked the door shut. I felt sorry for her, lying on the floor with her head by the umbrella stand, so I pulled her a little farther to the base of the stairs and arranged her in a half-upright position. It *was* underwear around her neck, a pink pair. Not a girl's, either. She also had a collection of swizzle sticks poking out of her hair, all different colors. She tried to wipe her hand across her face, hit her nose, then left her hand there and whimpered softly.

It had been a long time since I'd seen Ashley drunk. In her wilder years, back in high school, she was always getting busted coming in past curfew with a mouthful of Certs and her speech slurred. My mother was never taken in. The next morning Ashley would be grounded with a hangover, and my mother would vacuum outside the bedroom door bright and early, making a point of banging the vacuum against the wall in an effort to get those hard-to-reach spots. I'd woken up more than once to the sound of Ashley getting sick in the bathroom at two A.M., which she thought she was so cleverly hiding by running the shower and the exhaust fan. My parents were never fooled, not even for a minute. They locked their liquor cabinet and did a sniff test every night and eventually Ashley grew out of it, just like she did football players and short shorts and Sumner, not necessarily in that order. Lewis wasn't a drinker, or a druggie, or even bad tempered. Lewis was viceless, and Ashley gave up everything to become bland, just like him. At least, until tonight. Maybe her friends had known that this was her last gasp, her last chance at the wildness she'd once been famous for. Now I looked at my sister, prone at the bottom of the stairs, and thought how I would miss her when she was gone.

"Ashley." She still had her hand over her face, her eyes shut now. I reached down and shook her shoulder. "Come on, at least get on the couch." I crouched beside her, my tiny sister, and put an arm around her shoulders, helping her to her feet. We stumbled together into the living room, where I directed her to the couch and covered her with a blanket, taking off her one shoe and removing the swizzle sticks from her hair one by one. I left the underwear, just out of spite for all the times she'd been nasty to me in the last few months. Some things are deserved, between sisters.

I went to the kitchen and got a trash can, which I put by her head in case things got nasty later, and just as I was leaving to go upstairs she mumbled something, then said louder, "Hey."

"What?" She was just a blob on the couch now, in the dark. On the coffee table, by the swizzle sticks, I could see a pile of my mother's lists, all on yellow sticky paper, lying in the one slant of light that was coming in through the curtains.

"Come talk to me," she said, and I heard the couch creak as she slowly rolled over. "Haven."

I sat down on the chair beside the couch, pulling my legs up to my chest. I could remember when I'd fit in it perfectly, sinking into its deep cushions, when my feet didn't even touch the ground. Now I contorted myself, linking an elbow around a knee, just to fit in its small space. I didn't say anything.

"I'm gonna miss you, you know," she said suddenly, her voice clearer than before. "I know you don't believe that."

"I figured you couldn't wait to leave," I said.

She laughed, a long, lazy laugh. "Oh, yeah, I can't. I mean, I love Lewis. I love him, Haven. He's the only one who ever really cared about me."

This was old news. I nodded, knowing she couldn't see me in the dark.

"It's all gonna be okay, Haven. You know that, right? You know it." She was rambling now, her voice softer, then louder, falling off into sleep. "Mom and Dad and everything, it's all gonna be okay. And Lorna. And me and Lewis. We can't be sad about it forever, you know? We've got to think back to the good times, Haven, and just remember them; that's all we can do. We can't worry about the past or what happened at the end, anymore. I can't and you can't."

"I don't," I said softly, hoping she'd fall asleep.

"You do, though," she said quietly, her voice muffled by the blanket. "I can see it in your face, in your eyes. You gotta grow up, you know? It's nobody's fault. We had good times, don't you understand? Some people don't even have that."

I saw a shadow passing on the street outside, suddenly, and thought of Gwendolyn. Of going wild. I said, "Go to sleep, Ashley. It's late."

"We had good times," she murmured, more to herself now than to me, if she'd ever been talking to me, really. "Like that summer, at the beach. It was perfect."

"What summer?" I sat up now, listening closely. "Which one?"

"At the beach . . . you know. With Mom and Daddy, and the hotel, and playing Frisbee every night, all night. Remember, Haven? You have to remember that, and try to forget the rest. . . ." Her voice faded off, muffled.

"Sumner was there," I said to her, "remember, Ashley? Sumner was there the whole time and you guys were so great together, remember? He was the greatest."

"The greatest," she repeated in that same sleepy, soft voice. "It was the greatest."

"I didn't think you remembered," I said to her, leaning closer. "I thought you'd forgotten."

I waited, listening for her response, but she was out, her breathing steady and soft. "I thought you'd forgotten," I said again, quietly, before pulling the blanket tighter around her, smoothing my hand across her hair and sitting for a while in the dark, watching my sister dream.

The next morning Ashley spent three hours in the bathroom, moaning and flushing the toilet, while my mother and I stood outside the door wondering if we should intervene. Finally, in early afternoon, she emerged after a shower, looking kind of pasty but alive. Lewis showed up a half hour later, with Pepto-Bismol, ginger ale, and oyster crackers. He was quite a guy, that Lewis.

"I can't believe they just left me on the porch," Ashley was saying as I came into the kitchen later that afternoon. She and Lewis were at the table going over wedding details. She had her legs across his lap and he was rubbing her feet. "Some friends."

"They must have thought it would be funny," Lewis said in his soothing, even voice. He was wearing a pastel oxford shirt and madras shorts, a veritable explosion of color next to Ashley in her gray sweatpants and white T-shirt. She was nibbling on an oyster cracker, eating the edges.

"Well, it wasn't." She took another sip of ginger ale. "If it wasn't for Haven, I would have died, probably."

"No, you just would have woken up on the porch," I said.

"I'd rather die. Can you imagine what the neighbors would think?" Overnight, my sister had grown old again, worried about consequences. I missed the loopy silliness of her the night before, hanging off my arm with her hair in her face.

"Well, if you hadn't gone out drinking, and done what I did . . . ," Lewis said in a tsk-tsk voice, checking something off the list.

"Shut up," Ashley said, rearranging her feet in his lap.

"What did you do?" I asked, pulling out a chair and sitting down beside them.

"We went to a dinner, and then a baseball game," Lewis said smugly, "where I had two beers, and made it to my own bed without incident."

"And without underwear around your neck," I chimed in, reaching for an oyster cracker.

Suddenly I knew, without even looking up, that I'd said something wrong. Very wrong. I had the sensation of eyes boring into my neck, hard. As I lifted my head Ashley was staring at me, her mouth twisted in that tight line that meant I was in trouble.

"Underwear?" Lewis said, turning to face her. "What's this about underwear? I never heard anything about underwear."

"It's nothing," Ashley said, shooting me a death look.

"Underwear is not nothing," Lewis said, shifting in his chair so that her feet fell out of his lap to the floor. "You said you just went to dinner and had too many margaritas. You didn't say anything even remotely related to underwear."

"Lewis, please," Ashley said. "We went to this place, right before we came home. We didn't stay long, it was stupid, but they told the guy I was getting married and then he . . ."

"Oh, God," Lewis said, throwing down his pencil. "Strippers? You were with strippers last night?"

"Not strippers, Lewis," Ashley said in a tired voice. "They're exotic dancers, and I didn't even want to go. It was Heather's idea."

"I don't believe this." Lewis looked at me, as if I could help, and I looked back at the table. "We promised each other we wouldn't do any of that traditional stuff, Ashley. You made a vow."

"Lewis, don't do this. It was just a stupid thing."

Lewis crossed his legs, a habit that always made my father cringe. "Did you touch him?"

Ashley sighed. "Not really."

There was a silence and I thought about making a quick exit, but as I moved to go I felt Ashley's foot lock around the bottom of my chair, holding it in place.

"Not really," Lewis repeated slowly. "So that would be a yes."

"It wasn't like I *touched* him," Ashley said quickly, "but he danced in front of me and I had to put money in his . . . , thing . . . because it's rude if you . . ."

"His thing?" Lewis shrieked. "You touched his thing?"

"His underwear," Ashley said. "God, Lewis, his underwear, for Christ's sake."

"The same underwear that was around your neck, right?" Lewis stood up, pushing his chair out. "I don't want to hear about this, okay? A week before my wedding and my fiancée is out putting her hands on strange men . . . I just can't think about it right now."

"Lewis, don't be like this," Ashley said, too tired and hung over to get into a big fight. "Like I said, it's just a dumb thing."

"Well, obviously *that* vow didn't mean much to you," Lewis snapped. "So I wonder if any of the others will."

"Oh, please," Ashley said, rolling her eyes. "I'm too tired to deal with your dramatics, Lewis. Let's just forget about it."

Lewis just looked at her, in his pastels and madras. "I think I need some time away from you, Ashley. I have to go now." And with that he walked stiffly to the door, opened it, and left with a great flourish of shutting it behind him. Ashley just watched him go, then turned her gaze on me.

"Thanks a lot, Haven," she said icily. "Thanks a whole lot." She stood up and slammed her glass on the table, then went out the same door, calling his name.

I sat at the table knowing I should feel bad. But I couldn't do it. I knew I owed Ashley somewhere for something nasty she'd done to me; there had been enough over the years. It was exhilarating in a way, this feeling of wrongdoing, of making things even. I listened to them arguing outside and thought of Ashley the night before, telling me to remember when things were good. I sat back, listening, and concentrated on this moment, my last act of revenge against my sister, and savored it.

It was later that night that I got the call from Casey. I didn't even recognize her voice at first, a voice I'd heard all my life. She sounded like she was choking, or had a cold.

"I need to talk to you," she said as soon as I picked up the phone where Ashley had left it dangling on the floor with a glare at me. She was still mad, even though Lewis had forgiven her before he even made it down the driveway. "It's important."

"Okay," I said. "Should I come over?"

"No," she said quickly, and in the background I could hear baby Ronald hollering. "Meet me halfway. Right now, okay?"

"Sure." I hung up, found my shoes, then walked to the living room, where my mother, Lydia, and Ashley were watching "Murder, She Wrote" and making lists. "I'm going for a walk with Casey."

"Fine." My mother hardly looked up, her mind on the band and the ushers and the flower arrangements. "Be back by ten."

As I stepped into the thick summer air I heard only cicadas, screaming from the trees around our house. It was warm and sticky and I left my shoes on the porch, walking barefoot down the sidewalk, past houses with their lights burning, the sound of televisions drifting from open windows. I could see Casey coming from the other direction, walking quickly and brushing her hair out of her face. We met halfway, by the mailbox in front of the Johnsons'.

"It's horrible," she said to me, breathless. She was sniffling—no, crying—and she kept walking, with me falling into step behind her. "I just can't believe it."

"What?" I'd never seen her like this.

"He broke up with me," she said, sobbing. "That bastard, he broke up with me over the phone. Just a few minutes ago."

"Rick?" I pictured him from all those packs of glossy three-by-fives, always grinning into the camera, a stranger from Pennsylvania.

"Yes," she said, wiping her nose with the back of her hand. "I have to sit down." She plopped herself on the curb and pulled her knees to her chest, burying her face in her hands.

"Casey." I reached to put my arm around her, unsure of how to act or what to say. This was the first time it had happened to us. "I'm so sorry."

"I'd been calling so much, but he was never home, right? And I was leaving all these messages. . . ." She stopped and wiped her eyes. "And his mother kept saying he was out, or busy, and finally he called me back today and said she made him call me. Haven, he'd been telling her all along to say he wasn't home. He just didn't want to talk to me."

"He's a jerk," I said defensively, hearing that judging tone in my own voice, the one I recognized from Lydia Catrell talking to my mother all those mornings.

"He was hoping I'd just lose interest. . . . He didn't even have the guts to call me and tell me he had a new girlfriend. He had his mom lying to me, Haven." She made little hiccuping noises, bumpy sobs. I kept patting her shoulder, trying to help. "God, I was so stupid. I was going to go up there."

"He's an asshole." I could see Rick, someone I didn't

know, lurking at the end of a telephone line, mouthing the words *I'm not here.* I hated Rick, now.

"It's so awful," she said, resting her head against my shoulder and sobbing full strength, while I cupped my arm around her head and held her close. "It hurts."

I'd never been in love, never felt that surge of feeling or that fall from its graces. I'd only watched as others weathered it; my mother in her garden, Sumner on the front lawn all those years ago, Ashley sobbing from the other side of a wall. I sat curbside with my best friend, Casey Melvin, and held her, trying to shoulder some of the hurt. There's only so much you can do, in these situations. We sat there together in our neighborhood and Casey cried, a short distance down from halfway.

Chapter Eleven

We were down to three days and counting. Things around the house were getting crazy, with the phone ringing off the hook and travel arrangements for the incoming relatives and Ashley having a breakdown every five seconds, it seemed. My mother and Lydia had set up headquarters at the kitchen table, with all the lists and plans and last-minute invitations covering the space entirely. I had to sit on the counter, with the displaced toaster oven, just to get my Pop-Tart in the morning.

Meanwhile, the rest of the world went on, although it was hard to imagine how. Casey was still suffering, having locked herself in her room and refused to eat for three days, until her mother took her shopping, got her hair permed, and signed them up for another tap-dancing class. Life would go on for Casey, with Rick retreating to just pictures in a photo album.

My father and Lorna had returned from a News Channel 5 promotional trip to the Bahamas, where they'd accompanied a group of viewers who'd won a contest involving sports and weather trivia. My father came back with even more hair, a sunburn, and a set of shell windchimes for me, which I hung outside my bedroom window, where it clanged all night until Ashley claimed it was ruining her sleep and demanded I take it down. I did, but I resented it. I resented everyone lately.

It had started soon after Ashley's bachelorette party and Casey's dumping. It was a feeling I'd woken up with one morning, a kind of whirring in my ears and an instability of the world, like things were coming to a head. I faced myself in the bathroom mirror and looked into my eyes, wondering if I would see something new in them, something crackling and different. I felt strong, as if every muscle in my body was taut and lean, not creaky and bony anymore. As if I was growing into myself, finally. I heard things differently, the sound of the neighborhood and the cicadas at night and my own breath, even and full. Everything was heightened, from the blazing blue of the sky to the feel of slippery grass under my feet to the sound of my mother's voice calling my name from across a room. It was both scary and exhilarating, unsettling and amazing.

The day before Ashley's wedding was also the first

day of the Lakeview Mall Hot Summer Deals Sidewalk Sale, which basically consisted of all the stores taking all the junk they couldn't sell and putting it outside, slashing the prices in half, and then watching as shoppers gobbled it up. I had to be at work extra early, at seven A.M., to help put one half of every ugly pair of shoes from the storeroom on a table out front, where it was my job to stand and watch for shoplifters while my boss, Burt, shuffled back and forth to the storeroom to find the mates for the shoes on the table. It was loud and crazy in the mall, with people digging through all the merchandise and pushing up against me in their mad dash to find a bargain. But even in all this craziness—with Burt saying in my ear that my sock quota was low so Push Socks, Push Socks and the mall Muzak blaring Barry Manilow and all the hands, all colors and sizes, grabbing at the shoes in front of me—I felt that eerie calmness, that floating feeling, that had followed me for the last few days. It was like I was just above it all, hovering, and nothing affected me.

Out of the blue, a woman grabbed my hand and said, "You call twenty bucks for a kid's shoe a good deal?" She was wearing a bathing suit with shorts over it, flip-flops, and a big straw hat.

I just looked at her.

"Do you?" She picked up a shoe, one that was yellow and blue and pink, with what looked like Smurfs on it. "I'll give you ten bucks for this pair. If you have a five and a half."

"I don't know . . . ," I said, looking for Burt, who had

disappeared for a bathroom break a good twenty minutes ago. "We don't really bargain on shoes."

"You don't, huh?" she said in a nasty voice, like I'd been rude to her. "Well, that's just fine. Just find me a five and a half, would you?"

Burt appeared next to me now, smelling like the hand soap we used in the bathroom. "Is there a problem here, Haven?"

"Five and a half," the woman said loudly, shaking the shoe in my face. I watched the Smurfs blur past, blue and pink and yellow.

"Find the woman a five and a half," Burt said to me, prodding me in the back with one hand. "I'll deal with the table for a while."

I went back in the storeroom and climbed up to the discount shelf, looking for the ugly Smurf shoe. There was a six and a four but no five and a half, of course. I went back out to the table.

"Sorry, it's not in," I said.

"It's not in," she repeated flatly. "Are you sure?"

"I am indeed," I said, realizing that I was being a smartass and not really caring. Burt was looking at me. I felt that whooshing in my ears, that powerful evenness. I imagined myself floating down the Lakeview Mall, tied to nothing, the silk of those banners brushing my shoulders.

"Haven, perhaps you can interest the woman in another style," Burt said to me quickly.

"I want this one," the woman said, shaking the shoe in front of my face again. Behind her, someone else was saying, "Miss? Miss? I need some help with this shoe, please?"

"We don't have that shoe in, ma'am," I repeated to her in a singsong voice, my customer-pleasing smile stretching across my face.

"Well, then, I think I should get another shoe at the same price." She put one hand on her hip and I watched as the fabric of her bathing suit scrunched, folding over itself at her stomach. People just shouldn't wear beach attire in public. "It's only fair."

"Ma'am, it's a sale item, we're out of that size, and I'm sorry," I said, but already my mind was drifting. Burt was busy untying a bunch of shoelaces and the people were all around me and the Muzak in the mall seemed louder, suddenly. I wondered if I was going to pass out, right there in the middle of the Hot Summer Deals Sidewalk Sale.

"Well, that's just fine," the woman snapped. I watched as she tossed the shoe at me. She meant for it to hit the pile probably, but it bounced off a stray saddle shoe in the bin and nailed me in the head, a direct Smurf hit. I was hot all of a sudden, the whooshing in my ears loud and calming, and I felt awake, my skin tingling.

She was walking away, flip-flops thwacking against the floor, as I grabbed the shoe, ducked around the table, and went after her. I could still feel where the shoe had hit me, but that wasn't what spurred me on and made me rush through the crowd of bargain hunters, following the pudgy lady in the straw hat. It was something more, a giant mass of Ashley's snide remarks and tantrums, of

Lorna Queen's tiny ears and my father's new hair, of Sumner standing on our front lawn, abandoned, all those years ago. It was the tallness and Casey's Rick and Lydia Catrell and Europe, and my mother standing in the doorway watching me leave for my father's wedding. It was the whole damn summer, my whole damn life, leading up to this moment with this stranger in the middle of the Lakeview Mall.

"Excuse me," I said loudly as I came up behind her, gripping the shoe in my hand so tightly that I could feel the plastic ends of the laces pressing into my palm. "Excuse me."

She didn't hear me, so I reached forward and tapped her shoulder, feeling the smooth rubberiness of the bathing suit beneath my finger. She turned around.

"Yes?" Then she saw it was me, and her eyes narrowed, nasty.

I just looked at her, not sure at all what words would come out of my mouth. We were in the middle of the mall now by the giant gumball machine where the ceiling is high and glass. The sunlight was pouring in across the center court, hot and so bright I was squinting. The noises and voices were loud and rising above me, pushing their way to the skylight and the world outside. People were rushing by and the banners were floating above me as I faced this woman, this stranger, every inch of me tingling, electric.

"You forgot this," I said to her, in a voice that didn't sound like me, and threw the shoe back at her, hard, and stood watching as it hit her square in the forehead, the same spot where it had hit me. Then it fell to the floor, bounced once, and landed upright, as if it was waiting for a little foot to wiggle into it.

She was stunned, staring at me open-mouthed. She had gold fillings on two back teeth. I noticed this offhand as the crowds pressed around us and the sun beat down and I was suddenly tired, sure I'd never make it the short distance back to the store.

"I'll have you fired," she snapped, squatting down to grab up the shoe, and then added on the way back up, "and I'm calling mall security and reporting this. This is an assault." She looked around at the few people who had seen me throw a shoe at this woman, and pointed to each of them as she added, "Witnesses! You are all witnesses!"

Everyone was looking at me, suddenly, and the place was too bright, and so hot, and all I could see was her face and her open mouth, yelling. I spun around, reaching out like a blind person in the hot glare of that skylight, pushing people aside, and I began to run. I ran down the middle of the Lakeview Mall with those banners swishing overhead, seeing the shocked expressions of people as they jerked out of the way, yanking children and strollers aside. I could hear her yelling behind me, but I didn't care, couldn't think of anything as I burst out the main doors into the parking lot and kept running, my feet pounding the pavement. I wondered if this was how Gwendolyn felt, searching the streets for some kind of peace. If at fifteen she'd ever felt the same way, tall and lost, not fitting in or finding a place for herself, anywhere.

I was still running, nearing the edge of the parking lot that led to the road home, when I thought I heard someone—Sumner—yelling my name. I couldn't stop, not even for him, as I took the turn and headed into my neighborhood, slowing my pace and breathing heavily, the wind swirling in my ears.

I found myself at the neighborhood park, still trying to figure out what had come over me. I walked past the swings and the jungle gym to what was called the Creative Playground, built by a bunch of hippie parents when I was in grade school. It was made of wood, with slides and hiding places, and tires stacked one on top of the other creating vertical tunnels. I crawled underneath the main slide and folded myself small, as small as I'd been in second grade when I first discovered this space. I barely fit now, my knees at my chin, but it was mossy and quiet and somehow right then it seemed like the perfect place to be.

I was fired, obviously. No more Push Socks, Push Socks. I took off my name tag and stuck it in my pocket, wondering what kind of charges would await me when I got home. I wondered if you could get arrested for an assault with a Smurf shoe at a mall. If I'd go to jail. If I *could* go home.

But soon I wasn't thinking about that anymore, or about the woman or the Hot Summer Deals Sidewalk Sale. I leaned my head against the slippery wood behind me and thought of better times, of that summer in Virginia Beach. I thought about Sumner running through the sand, chasing a Frisbee as it flew over his head.

About the way he made Ashley human and shrimp cocktail at the hotel restaurant and my father's pink cheeks, his grinning as he slid an arm around my mother's waist, pulling her close. I thought of Ashley's high, singsong laugh and that ride down in the Volkswagen with beach music on the radio and the stars overhead, the summer so new with so many days left, each sliding into the next. I wished I could go back somehow and start it all over again, with me and Ashley by the curb waiting and listening for the putt-putt of the Bug to come around the corner. I'd live each of those days the exact same way, when I was no bigger than a minute. When my parents were still in love and Sumner held us all together, laughing, until the day Ashley sent him away without even thinking of what would happen once he was gone. No more laughing, no more drawing together from the opposite sides of the house, all coming together to Sumner's voice, his laugh. I missed who we all were then. One summer and one boy, and suddenly things weren't the same.

I walked home. I'd fallen asleep under the slide, dozing off in the mossy quiet, only to wake up confused, having forgotten where I was, the sun slanting down hot on my head. Some little boys were sliding down above me, their voices high and giggly, calling out to their father to watch. He was wearing sunglasses, reading a paper by the tire tunnel, and looked up each time they told him to. I waited until they were gone before I slipped out and unfolded myself to my true size.

I went into the house through the back door, hoping

to avoid seeing anyone; but of course there was another power meeting going on at the table, with Lydia and my mother hunched over the clipboard that seemed attached to my mother's hand lately and Ashley sitting in the doorway that led to the living room.

"Well, obviously we'll have to replan the whole wedding party," my mother was saying as I stood on the other side of the glass, invisible. "We can't have five ushers and four bridesmaids. Somebody's got to go."

"I've seen it done before," Lydia said, tugging at her sequined shirt. "Four bridesmaids, three ushers. But it never looked right to me. You need symmetry in a wedding party. You've just got to have it."

"I still cannot believe this," Ashley grumbled into her hair, which was hanging down one side of her face. "I'm going to kill her, I swear."

"There's no time to think about that now," Lydia said in her loud, brassy Floridian voice. "We can hate Carol later; now we've got to come up with some kind of a solution. Quickly."

"Okay," my mother said, flipping through some pages on her clipboard. "How's this: we just find another bridesmaid. Ashley, you could ask one of your friends, right?"

"Mother," Ashley said in that annoyed voice that I'd heard way too much of in the last six months, "the wedding is tomorrow."

"I know that," my mother said wearily.

"There's no time to get a bridesmaid, get a dress, get it fitted. . . . We can't do it. There's no way." Ashley picked at the fringe of her cutoffs.

"How about bumping an usher?" Lydia suggested. "There's got to be somebody we can ask to bow out. For the sake of evenness."

"We can't throw someone out of the wedding," Ashley said. "God, that would be so horrible. 'Oh, thanks for renting the tux and everything, but we won't be needing you. Get lost.'"

"Of course we wouldn't say it like that," Lydia said sullenly, and they all got quiet, their minds working this over.

I figured this was the best time of any to come in, so I headed straight across the kitchen, over Ashley in the doorway, and made a quick dash for the stairs.

"Haven?" My mother was already after me. I heard her pushing her chair away from the table, that familiar scrape, and then her footsteps coming down the hallway behind me. "Haven, I have to talk to you."

I stopped in the middle of the stairs and turned to look down at her. She seemed very small. "What is it?"

"Well," she said, starting to climb up, step by step, "I got a strange call from Burt Isker. Did you have some sort of problem at work today?"

"No," I said, turning back around and taking the rest of the stairs, then heading to my room only a few paces away.

"Whatever happened, we can talk about it," she said quietly, still following me. I felt that stab of guilt, but pushed it away because I was tired of protecting her from my father, forgiving him for leaving us for the pregnant Weather Pet, giving Ashley free reign to hurt me because she was The Bride.

"I don't want to talk about it," I said, and even as the words came out I knew the look I'd see if I turned around, the hurt like a slap spreading across her face. But I didn't turn around, didn't even stop walking, until I was in my room with my hand on the back of the door, closing it.

"Haven," my mother said in a louder voice, trying to be stern, "we're going to talk about this. If you're accosting the customers and running out on your job, obviously something is going on that we need to discuss. Now I know it's been hard this summer with the wedding, but this isn't—"

"It's not about the wedding. It's not about the goddamn wedding or Ashley. For once this isn't about her. It just isn't," I said, now looking at her face closely as it changed from authoritative to lost. And then I slammed the door in my mother's face, so hard it shook the pictures in their frames on the wall of my room. I could hear her breathing on the other side of the door, waiting for me to open it, apologize, pull her close, and save her from everything just like I always did. But I didn't. Not this time.

A few minutes later, as if conceding defeat, she just said, "Well, don't forget your father is coming over. You told him you'd go shopping with him for a gift for your sister." Her voice was soft, and she was trying to sound like she wasn't upset. She waited another minute, as if this might bring me out, and then I heard her going slowly down the stairs.

I walked to my bed and stretched out across it, symmetrical, with my feet pressed to the bedposts and my head locked against the headboard. I closed my eyes and tried to block it all out, the mall and the bathing-suit woman and my mother's face as the door swung to close on her. I tried to think about anything to block out the sound from my vent, so clear, and what I knew they'd be saying about me as soon as my mother got back downstairs.

"What's wrong?" That was Ashley.

"Nothing." My mother didn't sound like herself, her voice quiet and even. "Let's get back to this bridesmaid problem."

"What did she say to you?" Ashley said, protective now. "God, what is her problem lately? She's impossible to deal with. I swear, it's like she's purposely doing it so close to the wedding just to ruin it. . . ."

"It's not about the wedding," my mother said quietly, echoing my own words. "Just leave it alone, Ashley. You've got enough to worry about."

"I just think she could wait to have her nervous breakdown until next week. I mean, it's not like we don't have enough on our hands, and it's pretty selfish, really."

"Ashley," my mother said in a louder voice, sounding tired. "Leave it alone."

I lay there and listened as they talked about Carol, the difficult bridesmaid, who was supposed to fly in that afternoon but apparently had called earlier to say she had broken off her own engagement just this morning and was therefore too hysterical to attend. They went round and round, coming up with plan after plan, none of which would work. I looked at the clock. It was only eleven-fifteen.

And I was still expected to go shopping with my

father, to pick out the Perfect Gift for the Perfect Wedding. It was too late to cancel; my father had his faults, but he was always punctual. I went to my bathroom and washed my face, looking at myself under the greenish fluorescent light. I looked sick, haunted, which I felt was appropriate so I just left my face as it was, without applying any makeup or touching my hair. I was still in my work clothes as I crept downstairs, and out onto the porch to wait for him.

I heard the car before I saw it, the purring of the engine as it zipped around the corner and onto my street. He pulled up in front of the house like he always did and then beeped twice. I sat in the swing, watching him without moving. I wasn't sure if he could see me.

He sat in the car a few minutes longer, fiddling with the radio and smoothing his hand over his new hair. He beeped again. Still I sat there. I wanted him to come up to the house. I wanted him, I realized, to finally approach it and cross that imaginary line that had been drawn the day he packed a suitcase and left while I was at school, taking with him all his sports stuff and clothes and the stereo, which left a big hole on the wall of the living room. I wanted to watch him walk up the front steps, across the lawn he'd kept so neatly mowed all those years, to our front door and to be a man about it, not a coward who sat in his shiny new car at the curb, outside it all. I sat and watched my father, daring him to do it. To come claim me as he'd never done since that day, not lurking on the outskirts of what had once been shared property, waiting for me to cross the line myself, the line I hadn't even drawn.

He beeped again, and I saw my mother's face appear in the window beside the door, peering out at him. He backed up and turned the car around in our driveway, his head still craning to see if I'd appear—*whoosh*—suddenly, like a bouquet of roses from a magician's hand. My mother held the curtain aside, watching. I watched too, hidden in the shadows of our porch, as he slowly pulled out, coasted by with one last searching look, and then gunned the engine before disappearing. *Whoosh.*

Chapter Twelve

The first thing I felt when I woke up was that it was hot. Very hot. It was the middle of August and every day was hot, but there was something about that day that made it stand out. I'd napped without covers, having kicked off my light blanket and sheet, but still felt sticky and warm even with my fan pointed right at me. Outside, the sun was still blazing. I'd woken from a bad dream, one of those confusing ones where nobody is who they start out to be. Someone was leading me down my street, showing me things. First it was Lewis, in one of those skinny ties, but then his face changed to Sumner's. Then, as I turned away and then back, it switched again, to Lydia Catrell's, only she was very old and tiny, hunched over, and shrinking before my eyes. I woke up suddenly, confused, and remembered everything that had happened earlier in one great rush of colors and images flying past in a blur. I curled up smaller, pulling my pillow in close, and buried my face. This had been the longest day of my life. Everything was loaded with consequences, the wedding and the weeks to come; I wanted to sleep through it all. But the sun was spilling through the window, shiny and hot, and it was already one o'clock. It felt like forever since I'd climbed into bed after my father drove away, locking my bedroom door and ignoring my mother's voice as it whispered in the hallway outside. The earlier part of the day was fuzzy and distant, like the dream that was fading quickly from my head.

I stayed in bed for another hour, listening to the noises of my house. I heard Ashley next door, rustling around, doing the last bits of packing. Every once in a while it would get very quiet, and I wondered if she'd stopped to think about leaving. I wondered if she was sad. Then I'd hear her taping another box shut or making another trip downstairs, dragging something behind her. My mother and Lydia were in the kitchen, their voices high and chatty, against the tinkling of teaspoons and that humming excitement of something big getting ready to happen. I lay in my bed, feet to bedposts, head pressed to headboard. I lay as still as possible, pushing my back into the damp sheet beneath me. And I tried to think of the quiet that would come later, after tomorrow and the honeymoon and Europe, when there would be only me and my mother treading these floors and everything would be different.

I got up and showered, ran my hands across my body under the stream of water. Since I'd grown taller I hated looking down at myself; at my skinny legs, the knees poking out; my big feet splayed flat against the floor like clown shoes, ten sizes too big. But now I drew myself up to full height, pulling in a breath that spread through me. I thought of giraffes and stilts, of my bones linked carefully together. Of height and power, and gliding over the heads of the Lakeview Mall shoppers to touch those fluttering banners. As I stepped out to face myself in the mirror, reaching a hand to smooth away the steam, I saw myself differently. It was as if I had grown again as I slept, but this time just to fit my own size. As if my soul had expanded, filling out the gaps of the height that had burdened me all these months. Like a balloon filling slowly with air, becoming all smooth and buoyant, I felt like I finally fit within myself, edge to edge, every crevice filled.

"Hey," Ashley called out as I passed her open door on my way downstairs. "Haven. Come here a second."

I went in, immediately aware of how small her room looked with the dresser almost bare; the closet door open revealing empty shelves and racks; the bright spots of wallpaper where things had hung contrasting now to the faded rest of the wall. She was standing by her bed, folding a dress over one arm. She said, "I need to talk to you."

I stood there, tall, waiting.

She looked closer at me, as if she'd suddenly realized something she'd missed before. "Are you okay?"

"Yeah," I said. "Why?"

"You look different." She put the dress down in a box at her feet, kicking it shut. "Do you feel okay?"

"I'm fine."

She was still watching me, as if I couldn't be trusted. Then she shrugged, letting it go, and said, "I want to talk to you about earlier."

"What about it?"

"Haven," she said in that voice that meant she was feeling much, much older than me, "I know it's been hard for you with the wedding and all, but I'm concerned about how you treated Mom. It's hard enough for her right now without you freaking out and turning on her."

"I'm not freaking out," I said curtly, moving back towards the door.

"Hey, I'm not through talking to you," she said, walking quickly to block my path. I looked down at her, realizing how short she really was. She was in shorts and a red T-shirt, with a gold chain and matching earrings. "See, that's just what I'm talking about. It's like all of a sudden you just don't care about anyone but yourself. You snap at Mom, and now this attitude with me. . . ."

"Ashley, please," I said in a tired voice, and noticed how much I sounded like my mother.

"I'm just asking you to keep whatever is bothering you to yourself, at least until after tomorrow." She had her hand on her hip now, classic Ashley stance. "It's very selfish, you know, to pick these few days for whatever adolescent breakdown you're choosing to have. Very selfish."

"I'm selfish?" I said, and found myself actually throwing my head back to laugh, Ha! "God, Ashley, give me a break. As if everything in the last six months hasn't revolved around you and this stupid wedding. As if my whole life," I added, the light, airy feeling bubbling back up inside me, "hasn't revolved around you and your stupid life." It didn't even sound like me, the voice so casual and cutting. Like someone else. Someone bold.

She just looked at me, the gold engagement ring glinting on the hand she was shaking at me. "I'm not going to let you do this. I'm not going to let you get me started on this day, because I have too much to deal with and I'm not in the mood to fight with you. But I will say this. You better grow up and get your shit together in the next five minutes or you will regret it, Haven. I have planned this day and done too much for too long for you to decide to ruin it purely out of spite." Her hand went back to her hip, her lip jutting out.

"Oh, shut up," I said in my bold voice, stepping around her and out the bedroom door, then going down the stairs before she even had a chance to react. I was floating, the air whooshing through my ears all the way to the kitchen, where I found my mother and Lydia drinking coffee. They both looked up at me as I came drifting in, with the same expression Ashley had when she'd first called me into the room: as if suddenly I was no longer recognizable.

"Haven?" my mother said, turning in her chair as I reached for the Pop-Tarts and broke open a pack. "Is everything okay?"

"Just fine," I said cheerfully, lining up my tarts on the rack of the toaster oven. Upstairs Ashley was banging around, boxes crashing to the floor.

My mother and Lydia exchanged looks over their coffee, then went back to watching me. I concentrated on the toaster oven. After a minute or so Lydia asked, "Why don't you sit down and eat with us?"

"Okay." I took my tarts out and then sat down across from them and started eating, aware that they were still staring at me. After a few seconds of self-conscious nibbling I said, "What? What is it?"

"Nothing," Lydia said quickly, shrinking back in her chair. I thought about my dream where she'd been tiny tiny tiny.

"You just seem upset," my mother said gently, scooting her chair a little closer to me to suggest allegiance. "Do you want to talk about it?"

"No," I said in the same gentle voice. "I don't." And I went back to my Pop-Tart, envisioning that tether stretched to the limit, fraying from the strain, and then suddenly snapping into pieces, no longer able to hold against the force of my pulling away from it. I looked at my mother, with the same hair and same outfit and same expression as Lydia Catrell's, and thought, You go to Europe. You sell this house. I don't care anymore. I just don't care.

"Haven," my mother said in a pleading voice, placing her hand over mine. "It might make you feel better."

I don't care, I don't care, I don't care, I was thinking, stuffing pieces of Pop-Tart into my mouth one by one by one. Her hand was hot and snug over mine as I pulled it away and pushed my chair out from the table. "I don't want to talk about it," I snapped as Lydia Catrell pulled further back in her chair. "I don't care, okay? I just don't care."

"Honey," my mother said, and I could tell by the strain in her voice she was really worried now.

"I'm sorry," I said to her, unable to meet her eyes. I ran to the back door and out into the garden, slipping across the pathway past the blazing colors and smells, the tendrils reaching out to touch my skin, the mix of everything so sweet and humid, thick and stifling. I hit the edge and kept going, down the street past the Melvins' and out of our neighborhood altogether, past the Lakeview Mall with all the cars lined up in its parking lot in nice, even rows. I was someone else, someone bold, my feet finding the ground beneath me as I thought only of putting distance between me and what I'd left behind.

I didn't know where to go, or what to do. I had no job and only three dollars in my pocket, so I spent an hour walking around downtown. I bought an orangeade and spent a half hour on a bench sipping it, wondering if there was ever going to be any way for me to go home. I imagined the house itself in pieces, brought to the ground by my bad attitude. I imagined a crisis meeting convening as I sat there in the park, with Ashley and Lewis and my mother and Lydia and my ex-boss Burt

Isker and my father and Lorna, all of them debating the question What on Earth Has Happened to Haven? Only Sumner would be on my side. Over the space of just one summer he'd managed to breathe life into me again, just as he had all those years ago. And now I was playing hooky from my life there on that bench, on the day before the biggest day of my sister's life, and I didn't even care. I imagined their faces as they sat around that table, voices clucking with concern. I was causing a Crisis.

I called Casey. She was off phone restriction and back in her mother's good graces after tap-dancing lessons and family therapy. When she heard my voice she said, "Hey, hold on. I'm switching phones."

I was at a pay phone, watching a crazy man talk to himself on the bench I'd just left. I held on.

"Haven."

"Yeah."

"What the hell is going on with you?" She sounded incredulous, even as she whispered. "Your mom called here three times already, looking for you. They're freaking out over there."

"She called you?" I said.

"She thought you'd come here. She told Mom everything, and I overheard. My mom talks so damn loud."

"What'd they say?" I was the center of serious mother talks.

"Well, your mom asked if you'd been around and my mom said no, so then your mom goes into this whole thing about you freaking out at work this morning and then fighting with Ashley and running out of the house, and she's just frantic because she thinks you must be on drugs or something, she's not sure. . . ."

"Drugs?" I repeated. "Did she really say that?"

"Haven," Casey said matter-of-factly, as if she knew so much about these things. "They think everything is drugs. They do."

"I'm not on drugs," I said, offended.

"Well, that's not the point. So apparently your sister is going ballistic and your mom and Lydia are combing the neighborhood looking for you and the rehearsal is at six-thirty and they think you might ditch that too, so it's just imperative that they find you before then."

"The rehearsal dinner," I said. Of course. I was a bridesmaid. If I hadn't been, I doubted an all-points bulletin would ever have been issued.

"So what is going on?" Casey demanded. "Where are you? Tell me and I'll come meet you."

"Nothing's going on," I said. "I'm on my way home." I didn't know if that was true, but I didn't want Casey meeting me. I liked this freedom and I wasn't ready to share it.

"Are you sure?" she asked, sounding disappointed.

"I'll call you later," I said.

"Wait. At least tell me what happened at work. Your mom said she thought you'd assaulted a customer or something—"

"Later," I said to her. "Okay?"

"Okay," she said sullenly. "But are you all right? At least tell me that."

"I am," I said. "I just have some stuff to work out."

"Oh. Okay. Well, call me if you need me. I'm just here practicing my tap dancing."

"I will. 'Bye, Case." I hung up and glanced around the small park I'd been hiding in. There were families out with their kids, college students throwing a Frisbee while a big, dumb-looking dog chased after it. I wondered if the Town Car was cruising the streets downtown, Lydia hoping to catch a glimpse of me so that I could be rustled up and dragged to the rehearsal dinner. I was throwing everything out of whack, and I knew it. I was like a fugitive, running from some indefinable force made up of my mother's worried eyes and Ashley's whining and Lydia's Town Car, sucking up my steps even as I took them. It was late afternoon now, and hotter than ever. My shirt was sticking to me and I needed somewhere better to hide.

I was standing at the crosswalk, squinting, when I heard it. That humming of a car, coming around the corner behind me and then down the street, with Sumner behind the wheel. He stopped at the light, too far away to hear me even if I'd had time to yell his name. The light changed and he pulled away, one hand balanced on the steering wheel, the other arm hanging down the side of the car, drumming his fingers. He took off, I watched him go, blending with the other traffic until he turned onto a side street just a little way down. I started walking.

I found him at the senior center, a small building at the end of a long street of minimalls and office complexes. Everything looked very new and very clean, as if it had been hastily assembled the day before. Sumner's car was parked right next to the door, in a space marked FRIENDS.

I pushed the door open and went inside, looking around. I was still in my fugitive mode, suspicious, as I passed a group of tiny old women, all of them hunched over and white haired. They wore shiny Nike walking shoes with their skirts and sweaters. As I passed by them, my eyes averted, I heard one say in a quiet, musical voice, "What a beautiful, beautiful girl."

I turned, trying to catch another glimpse, but they had vanished around a corner. I could hear the soles of their shoes brushing the floor and the sound of music just down the hallway. I kept walking, past rooms with walls of bright, happy colors like Easter eggs. In one a group of people were busy painting, each behind an easel. One man glanced over his shoulder at me as I passed, holding his paintbrush in midstroke. In front of him was a half-finished canvas showing a beach scene, the water a mix of a million different blues, the sky a blaze of oranges and reds. I passed a sunroom where a woman in a wheelchair was reading a book, the light slanting through a window just enough to make her almost transparent, and came to a large room with a high ceiling and a shiny floor. In one corner was a record player, and a man shuffling through albums, while in front of him about ten couples danced in slow, even time. A woman in a long blue dress had her eyes closed, her chin resting on the shoulder of her partner as he carefully twirled her. A man with a flower in his button-hole was bowing to his partner as she smiled and took his hand for another dance. And in the far corner, by a table lined with cups and a punch bowl, I saw Sumner, his head thrown back in a laugh as he led a small, wiry woman with a crocheted shawl around their part of the dance floor. The woman was talking, her cheeks red, and Sumner listened, all the while spinning her slowly around, his feet moving smoothly across the shiny floor. He was in a red dress shirt with a blue tie and old black oxfords. His jeans were rolled into uneven cuffs, and his shirttail hung loose over the waist. When the music stopped, the couples broke up and applauded while the record guy picked out another song. Sumner bowed to his partner and she smiled, pulling her shawl closer around her.

People were milling around now, pairing off into new couples, and Sumner hung back by the punch bowl, waiting until the new song had begun. Then he crossed the room to a woman in a yellow pantsuit who was standing by the record player, arms crossed and watching the dancers with a half smile on her face. He came up to her grinning, extended his hand, and asked her to dance. She ran a hand through her short white hair, then nodded once before taking his hand and following him onto the floor. He slipped an arm around her waist, old-time style, and they began a neat box step, one-two-three-four. The music was cheerful and happy and everyone was smiling in this shiny room, where time could stop and you could forget about aching joints and old worries and let a young, handsome boy ask you to dance. I stood in the doorway and watched Sumner charm this woman as he had charmed me, and my sister, so many years ago. And I saw him through several more songs, each time waiting until everyone else was paired off and picking a woman who was standing alone watching the others. A wallflower wanting to join in but with something stopping her.

After a half hour the record man leaned into a microphone and said in a deep voice, "Last song, everyone. Last song."

I waited for Sumner to repeat his ritual for this last dance on this summer afternoon. He skirted the edge of the dancers, flitting in and out of my sight, a red blur among the shifting shapes. Then he cut right through the crowd, past women with their eyes closed, lost in the music, and walked a slow, steady pace right to me. He held out his hand, palm up like expecting a high five, and said, "Come on, Haven. It's the last dance."

"I don't dance," I said, my face flushing when I noticed all the couples on the floor were looking at us with that proud, attentive look of grandparents and spinster aunts.

"I'll show you," he said, still grinning. "Come on, twinkletoes."

I put my hand into his and felt his fingers fold over mine, gently leading me to the edge of the floor. I was about to make some joke about how I dwarfed him but he put his arm around my waist and pulled me closer and suddenly I didn't feel like joking about anything. He held my hand and concentrated on the music before saying, "Okay. Just do what I do."

So I did. I've never been a dancer, always too clumsy and flailing. Dancing was for tiny girls and ballerinas, girls the size to be hoisted and dipped, easily enclosed in an arm. But as Sumner led me around the floor, my feet slowly getting used to the curve and glide of the steps, I didn't think about how tall I was, or how gawky, or how I stood so far over him, his head at my neck. I closed my eyes and listened to the music, feeling his arm around me. I was tired, after this long day and it suddenly seemed like I wouldn't even be able to stand up without Sumner there supporting me, holding my hand. The music was soaring, all soprano and harps and sadness, mourning some lost boy away at war, but still I kept my eyes shut and tried to remember every detail of this dance, because even then I knew that it wouldn't last. It was just a moment, a perfect moment, as time stood still and fleetingly everything fell back into its proper place. I let him lead me around the floor of the senior center and forgot everything but the feel of his shoulder beneath my hand and his voice, saying softly, "There you go, Haven. That's great. Can you believe it? You're dancing."

When the music stopped and I opened my eyes, all those elderly couples were grouped around us, applauding and smiling and nodding at each other, a silent consensus that what I'd felt wasn't just imagined. There was something special about Sumner, something that spread across rooms and years and memories, and for the length of a song I'd been part of it once again.

"So," he said once we were in his car and pulling out of the parking lot, "tell me what's wrong."

"Nothing," I said, holding my hand out and letting the warm air push through it as we went down the street, back to the boulevard.

"Come on, Haven." We were at a stoplight now, and

he turned to look at me. His eyes were so blue behind his glasses, which were lopsided. "I know what happened at the mall."

I kept my eyes on the light, waiting for the green. "That was no big thing," I said, trying to conjure up my bold self, to hear that whooshing again that made me rise above it all, immune. "I quit anyway."

He was still looking at me. "Haven. Don't bullshit me now. I know when something's wrong."

And still we sat, at what had to be the longest light in the world, with him staring at me until I finally said, "I'm just pissed off at Ashley, okay? And my mother and all this wedding crap." I sat back in my seat, balancing my feet on the dashboard the way I'd seen Ashley do all those years ago. "I really don't want to talk about it."

The light changed and we turned right, heading towards the mall and my neighborhood. "Well," he said slowly, shifting gears, "don't be so hard on Ashley. Getting married must be kind of stressful. She probably doesn't mean to take it out on you."

"It's not about the wedding," I said, realizing how tired I was of repeating these words and this sentiment. "God, Ashley did exist before this wedding, you know, and she was my sister a long time before she became the bride, and we have problems going way back that have nothing to do with this goddamn wedding anyway."

"I know she existed before this," he said gently. "I knew her once too, remember?"

"Yeah, but when you knew her she was different," I said. "God, Sumner, you made her different. You changed her."

"I don't know about that," he said. "It was high school, Haven. It was a long time ago."

"You made her happy," I told him. "With you she was nice to me and she laughed; God, she laughed all the time. We all did."

"It was a long time ago," he said again. This wasn't what I wanted from him; I'd expected sympathy, shared anger, something. Understanding and encouragement. I wanted him to rage with me against everything and everyone, but instead he just drove, saying nothing now.

We were getting closer to my neighborhood, and I said, "If you're planning to take me home you can just drop me off here. I'm not going."

"Haven, come on." He turned to look at me. Over his shoulder I suddenly noticed storm clouds, which seemed to have popped up from nowhere. They were long and flat, full of grays and blacks, and hadn't yet reached the sun blazing above us. "Your mom is probably worried about you and it's getting late. Just let me take you home."

"I don't want to go home," I said again, louder. "And it's only five-fifteen, Sumner. If you're going to take me home to my mother like I'm still eight years old, just stop the car and I'll get out here."

He pulled over to the side of the road, right next to the mall. "Okay, Haven. I won't take you home. But I'm not dumping you on the side of the road, either. So it's up to you what we do now."

We sat there, with cars passing and the sun beating down, while he watched me and I stared at my reflection in the side mirror. My face looked dirty and hot. "You don't understand." I wondered if I was going to start crying.

He cut off the engine and sat back in his seat, jiggling the keys in the ignition. "Understand what?" He sounded tired, fed up. This wasn't going the way I'd thought it would. I wanted to be back on that dance floor with his arm around me, surrounded by all those old, crinkly, smiling faces, safe and perfect.

"Any of this," I said. "You don't understand what's happened since you left."

"Since I left?"

"Since Ashley sent you away," I said, still focusing on my own face in the mirror, my own mouth talking. "That Halloween. A lot has changed."

"Haven . . . ," he said, drawing in a breath as if preparing to say something a parent would say, something sensible that cuts you off with the wave of one hand.

"My father ran off with the weathergirl, Sumner," I said, and suddenly the words were rushing out crazylike, jumbled and fast, "and Ashley didn't like me and my mother was so sad, it just broke her heart. And then Lydia moved in with her Town Car and Ashley found Lewis at the Yogurt Paradise and nobody was who they'd been before, not even me. When you left—when she sent you away—it was like that started it all. When you were there, remember, everything was still good. We were all happy, and then Ashley was such a bitch and she sent you away and everything fell apart, just like that. God," I said, realizing how loud my voice was, and how jagged I sounded, "it was just like *that*."

All this time he was staring ahead, Ashley's first

love in a wrinkled red shirt and Buddy Holly glasses. He shook his head, gently, and said to the road ahead, "There's a lot you don't understand, Haven. Ashley—"

"I don't want to hear about Ashley," I snapped, tired of her name and her face and the way she took over everything, even this moment, controlling it all. "I hate Ashley."

"Don't say that," he said. "You don't know." Now he sounded like everyone else, passing judgment, making assumptions. Not listening to me at this moment when it suddenly mattered so much.

"I know plenty," I said, because this sounded final. I wanted him to agree with me. To believe me. But he only sat there and shook his head, his fingers on his keys, as if the very words I'd said disappointed him.

The storm clouds were moving fast, piling into a dark heap that was spreading across the sky. The wind picked up, a hot breeze blowing across us, and I could smell the dirt and the road and my own sweat.

"It was her fault," I said quietly, seeing him again on the front lawn that Halloween, watching her window, "it was her fault you left. She sent you away."

"Haven, I can't deal with this," he said, hitting his hands on the steering wheel, suddenly angry. "I don't know what to say to you—"

"You don't have to say anything," I said, surprised to hear him raise his voice, lose patience with me. This wasn't how I remembered him.

"Look, Haven," he said, "what happened with me and Ashley . . . well, it wasn't like you remember it. There was a lot involved."

There always is, I wanted to tell him. These were the same things my mother said to me after my father left, trying to convince me it wasn't all the Weather Pet's fault.

"I've got to take you home," he said. The storm clouds were grouped high above us, black and foreboding with a blue sky peeking out behind. It was still sticky and hot, but the breeze was changing, now cooler and heavy, sending grass clipping swirling by the side of the road.

"I'm not going home," I said again as the clouds slipped over the sun, amazed at how fast the weather can change, a front blowing in a matter of minutes.

He started the engine, ignoring me, and put the car in gear. We slid away from the curb just as big fat drops began to fall, splashing across the windshield and my face. The cars coming towards us were turning their lights on, all at once. I opened my door and jumped out, slamming it behind me as my feet hit ground.

"Haven!" Sumner yelled at me, stopping the car again as I cut across the side of the road to a path, the back way we'd always taken to the mall to buy candy and Slurpees when I was little. "It's getting ready to pour; don't be stupid. Come on, get back in the car."

"No," I said softly, knowing he couldn't hear me. It was really raining now. I kept walking, hearing Sumner yell my name but knowing I couldn't go back to him, that he wasn't what I'd wanted him to be. Maybe he never had been.

As I got farther down the path I couldn't hear the traffic anymore, just the rain and thunder. I cut across a small creek, on a plank stretched across it, and saw the first flash of lightning shining suddenly above and then disappearing. It was followed by a crack of thunder that seemed to come from right behind me, pushing me forwards. The path was different than I remembered it, twisting around trees and rocks I didn't recognize, but then it had been a long time. Everything looks different when you're older, not staring up at the world but down upon it. Another clap of thunder boomed over me. I was sure the path came out in my neighborhood somewhere.

I couldn't see houses or lights, just trees followed by more trees, stretching into the distance. Suddenly I wasn't even sure if I was still on the path at all, and that made me panic and start to run, brushing branches out of my face as the rain pelted my back and dripped into my eyes, slippery and cold. The sky was black above me now and I started to think about tornados, the world swirling around and me with nothing to hold on to but trees, and this pushed me to run faster, the sound of my breathing hoarse in my ears. I couldn't see the path anymore in the rain and the dark, and everything was slippery beneath me as I ran harder, towards what had to be a clearing ahead. I thought of the houses on my street with their warm lights and the even, green lawns and all the landmarks, so familiar I could find them in my sleep. I ran to that clearing, sure that I could see it all in front of me—until I reached the last set of branches and pulled them aside to reveal more branches, and leaves dripping with rain, and pushed through with all my strength to burst out into open space, my heart racing in my chest, and kept running until I hit something, hard, something that moved and jumped back, its own breath hitting my face.

It was Gwendolyn.

She was sopping wet, her hair sticking to her forehead, in a white T-shirt with a red tank top showing through beneath and black running shorts. A pair of headphones hung around her neck, attached to a Walkman clipped to her waist. She was breathing hard, her face flushed and beaded with raindrops, and she was the first person I'd met in a long, long time who stood taller than me and looked down into my eyes. The thunder boomed around us, with another flash of white light, and Gwendolyn Rogers and I, breathing hard, stood still in that clearing, close enough that I could see the goose bumps on her flesh. She stared at me with her big, sad eyes as I stared right back, unflinching even when she raised her hand to my face and brushed her fingers across my cheek as if she wasn't sure I was real.

It seemed like we stood there together forever, Gwendolyn and I, two strangers in a clearing with the rain pounding down, inexplicably brought together in a summer storm. I wanted to talk to her, wanted words to come so I could say something that would make this all real. Something about what we had in common: a neighborhood, a summer, a revelation about a belief once considered sacred. But she only stared at me, her face wistful, a small smile creeping across it as if she knew me, had lost me along the way and only now found me again, here. I think she knew it too in that moment. She knew *me*.

Then I heard my sister's voice.

"Haven!" A car door slammed, hard, and then again, "Haven! Are you there?"

"I'm here," I said to Gwendolyn, and she pulled back from me, dropping her hand. I turned to look for my sister, who was still calling through the rain and the trees. "I'm here," I said again.

Ashley was coming through the brush now. She was bare-legged, wearing a yellow raincoat like the Morton Salt Girl, pulled tight. The trees were bending overhead, wind whistling through as the rain blew across me. I turned back around: Gwendolyn was already running down the path the way I'd come, a blur of white and black.

"Haven?" Ashley was closer now and I turned to the sound of her voice. Her raincoat was dripping wet, shiny and bright among all the green. I could see the headlights of her car now, beaming into the clearing. "Are you okay?"

"I'm fine," I said. "I got lost on this path."

"We were so worried," she said, coming to stand in front of me and wiping her hair out of her eyes. "Mom's practically hysterical calling everyone, and then Sumner Lee shows up and says you went running off into the woods back here."

"He talked to you?" I asked.

"He was worried too," my sister said, so small and wet in front of me. "We all were. God, Haven," she said softly, "what happened to you today?"

"I don't know," I said, and I was tired and wet, thinking only of crawling into my warm bed and putting this whole day behind me forever. But I had one more thing to say, to ask her, before I could do that. "Ashley."

"Yeah." She had turned to walk out of the clearing, and I faced the back of her raincoat.

"Why did you dump Sumner?"

She stopped and turned to face me. "What?"

"Sumner. Why did you break up with him that Halloween?"

"I dumped him?" she said. "Is that what he told you?"

"No," I said. "But I saw you do it. That Halloween when he was the mad scientist, remember? I saw you from the window."

"Haven," she said slowly, shaking her head. "I didn't dump Sumner. I mean, I did, but only because he cheated on me. With that girl Laurel Adams; remember her? I walked in on them that night at the party. That's why I broke up with him." She watched me as she said this, her voice even and sad. "All this time you didn't know, did you? God, Haven. He broke my heart."

I stood there and faced my sister, thinking back to that Halloween when I watched them driving down the street, Sumner in the front seat with Ashley beside him, and Laurel Adams in back with her hair shimmering silver under the streetlight. "That's not true," I said, thinking of Sumner as he held me on the dance floor earlier that afternoon. "It isn't."

"It is true. I loved Sumner and he hurt me badly." She reached up to brush my hair out of my face, an awkward gesture, a try at tenderness. "It's not always so simple, Haven. Sometimes there isn't a good guy and a bad guy. Sometimes even the ones you want to believe turn out to be liars."

"But he was so sad, and he kept coming around," I said, still not wanting to believe it was possible. "He begged for you to come back."

"That didn't change what he did." She shook her head, smiling sadly at me. "Haven, I know you don't like Lewis, but you have to understand how important it is to me to be able to trust someone I love. After Sumner and after Daddy, I was beginning to lose faith in everything. Lewis might not be Sumner, but he would never hurt me. Never. Sometimes things don't turn out the way you want them to, Haven. Sometimes the people you choose to believe are wrong."

"He loved you," I told her. "He still does, I think."

"He doesn't love me," she said, crossing her arms against her chest. "He might still love me as I was at fifteen, when I didn't know any better. When I trusted everyone. I'm not that person anymore." She started walking, holding aside the branches so I could get through. "He's just a boy, Haven. He was the first to really hurt me, but he's just a boy. There were a lot of them."

"Not like him," I said softly, although I knew that after today I'd never see him, or that summer at the beach, the same way.

"Maybe not," she said as we came to the car. "But maybe that isn't so bad. You can't love anyone that way more than once in a lifetime. It's too hard and it hurts too much when it ends. The first boy is always the hardest to get over, Haven. It's just the way the world works."

She held my door open for me as I climbed in, wet and sticky and tired after a day that was now a blur in my head, stretching back into forever. I watched her come around the front of the car and climb into the driver's seat and shut the door behind her. We didn't talk, me and my sister on the day before her wedding. She drove through the rain down those familiar streets, the houses all shiny and bright, and I thought about Sumner and that first summer, when everything was different. He'd affected both of us in separate but similar ways. He was the first to break her heart, and the first boy to let me down, to take something from me that I'd clung to so closely. A myth. Maybe Ashley was right, for once.

I thought about telling her this in the quiet of the car with only the rain drumming overhead. I looked over at her and thought better of it. Some things you don't have to tell. Some things, between sisters, are understood.

Chapter Thirteen

"*It's time.*" My mother was standing in my doorway, in a new pink dress with a corsage pinned below her right shoulder, a group of pink zinnias ringed with blue phlox. The entire house smelled like flowers that morning, from the bouquets that were lined up on the kitchen table, each constructed by her own hands.

I turned away from the mirror and she sighed, clasping her hands in front of her. "You look beautiful," she whispered, having broken into sobs so many times that morning that she had Kleenex poking out of her pocket, ready. "The dress is perfect. It looks just right."

Lydia Catrell popped into the doorway and promptly burst into tears. "You are a vision," she said, sniffling, as my mother offered her a damp Kleenex, which she waved away. "Isn't she something?"

"She is," my mother said softly, coming forward to hug me, her corsage pressing against my chest. She took my hand and we started down the stairs, with Lydia chattering ahead of us.

"I just know I'm going to bawl," she said loudly, the waterworks having passed. "I always cry at weddings, don't you?"

"I do," my mother said, squeezing my hand. "But Haven will be the strong one. Lucky for her she didn't inherit her mother's emotional tendency."

"Oh, there's nothing like a wedding for a good cry," Lydia said, clomping down the steps in her huge white slingbacks. "Everyone needs a good cry now and then."

My mother was still holding my hand as we walked through the hallway and out the door to the car. When I'd come home with Ashley she'd only hugged me so tight it hurt before letting me go upstairs for a shower and a long nap, skipping the rehearsal dinner altogether. When I woke up I found her and Ashley at the kitchen table, drinking wine and laughing, their voices drifting up like music. I sat in my nightgown and drank ginger ale with them, and we talked about the old times: when Ashley was ten and almost burnt the house down with her Easy-Bake oven, and when I was six and decided to run away, packing my red patent-leather suitcase with nothing but washcloths and underwear. My mother was laughing, her face flushed pink like it always was when she drank, telling the stories that for so long had remained in the no-man's land of the divorce, uncomfortable for what they no longer represented. Now we laughed about my father's hair and about Ashley's boyfriends, the timeline of boys, each with a quirk we remembered better than his name. And we laughed while it rained and the air smelled sweet blowing in the back door, like the flowers that bloomed just outside. The kitchen was warm and bright and I knew I would remember this night, in the same misty way I'd remembered all the good things, as a time when things were as perfect as they could be. Another summer to reach back to, that week in Virginia Beach now tucked away with the other, older memories. Later, when Ashley was gone and my mother and I tried to fill this house ourselves, I'd look back to that night and remember every detail, from Ashley's ring glittering as she sipped her wine to my mother's bare feet beside me on the chair, flecked with grass clippings. It would be a good place to start over.

I held my mother's hand as we walked to the car, knowing that things would be different now. My mother and I would have to start our own memories, maybe in a new setting. She'd go to Europe, because I'd make her, and I'd get another job, away from the mall, and start again with the fall and my junior year. My sister would be with Lewis and I would know that she was happy, there in her new apartment, without me on the other side of the wall. I'd have to let her go. And I would start my own timeline now, with the faces of my own boys marking the days and months and years.

I kept wanting to find Ashley, to tell her these things, but at the church it was crowded and crazy, with everyone running around and Ashley always behind a closed door or being whisked past in a blur of white. I stood in line with the other bridesmaids, Carol Cliffordson nowhere in sight, symmetry be damned. I held my bouquet and said I was fine, really, it was just a twenty-four-hour bug. I'd been a bridesmaid before: I knew what to do. And when the music started I stepped forward and followed the girl before me to the end of the aisle, past Casey and her parents and Lorna Queen and finally my mother and Lydia, all the while wishing I'd had time to say something to Ashley. Something about the day before, and how I was sorry. About how I would miss her and that I understood now about Sumner, and how he had brought us back together and given us something in common again. The night before, we'd been so caught up in the past that I couldn't make myself think ahead to this day and what came next, for either of us. I'd gone to bed and listened to her in the room beside me just as I had every other night of my life, not realizing that the next morning would be too late.

The organist started "Here Comes the Bride" and we all turned to the back of the church, expectant, and there she was. My father was grinning, his arm linked with hers as they took the first step together. Everyone was oohing and aahing because she was beautiful, white and gliding and perfect, and I watched her come towards me, a small smile on her face. I saw Lewis blushing and my mother dabbing her eyes and I thought about all we'd been through, my sister and I, the fights and the good times and every day we'd had that led up to this one and suddenly I was crying. I knew my mascara was running and I was the only one up there in front so close to bawling, but still the tears came, rolling down my cheeks as she got closer and her own eyes met mine from beneath her veil. I wanted to say it all then, but before I could speak she stepped away from my father and put her arms around me, hugging me tightly, her bouquet against my neck. I smelled flowers, my mother's garden, as I held her and knew I didn't have to say anything. My sister was wiser than I ever gave her credit for. She held me and whispered she loved me before pulling back, wiping her own eyes.

I knew it then. For me and Ashley, there wasn't any time left to think back to that summer and the beach and a boy who charmed us and disappointed us. There was only what stretched out ahead, years full of new summers and promise, with all the time in the world left to start again. My sister, who never understood most of the things I wanted her to, might have been able to understand what had happened to me in this summer of weddings and beginnings. And she was right. The first boy was always the hardest.